The blast rocked the warehouse

The Executioner hung the M-16 over his shoulder, filled his hands with the Blaster and caressed the trigger, sending the first missle streaking downrange with a loud chug.

As the toxic brew showered armed shadows charging for a nearby pocket, banshee shrieks flaying the air, Bolan jacked the handle, rotated another projectile into place and pumped out another hell bomb. No point in pulling punches, he decided, no sense fretting about noise and police swarming the block.

The Executioner was moving in to run and gun. Another batch of drums puked away toxic loads on a roaring ball of fire to douse a few more cannibals in what amounted to the fires of hell on earth.

There went the neighborhood.

MACK BOLAN
The Executioner

The Executioner
Don Pendleton's

TRIANGLE OF
TERROR

A GOLD EAGLE BOOK FROM
WORLDWIDE®

TORONTO • NEW YORK • LONDON
AMSTERDAM • PARIS • SYDNEY • HAMBURG
STOCKHOLM • ATHENS • TOKYO • MILAN
MADRID • WARSAW • BUDAPEST • AUCKLAND

First edition March 2006
ISBN 0-373-64328-4

Special thanks and acknowledgment to
Dan Schmidt for his contribution to this work.

TRIANGLE OF TERROR

Nothing can excuse a general who takes advantage of the knowledge acquired in the service of his country, to deliver up her frontier and her towns to foreigners. This is a crime reprobated by every principle of religion, morality and honor.

—Napoleon I, 1769–1821
Maxims of War

There is no lower form of treachery than to betray your fellow citizens in the name of greed and power. I will not rest while traitors plot their moves. I will be one step ahead of them and will make sure they get their due.

—Mack Bolan

THE
MACK BOLAN
LEGEND

Nothing less than a war could have fashioned the destiny of the man called Mack Bolan. Bolan earned the Executioner title in the jungle hell of Vietnam.

But this soldier also wore another name—Sergeant Mercy. He was so tagged because of the compassion he showed to wounded comrades-in-arms and Vietnamese civilians.

Mack Bolan's second tour of duty ended prematurely when he was given emergency leave to return home and bury his family, victims of the Mob. Then he declared a one-man war against the Mafia.

He confronted the Families head-on from coast to coast, and soon a hope of victory began to appear. But Bolan had broken society's every rule. That same society started gunning for this elusive warrior—to no avail.

So Bolan was offered amnesty to work within the system against terrorism. This time, as an employee of Uncle Sam, Bolan became Colonel John Phoenix. With a command center at Stony Man Farm in Virginia, he and his new allies—Able Team and Phoenix Force—waged relentless war on a new adversary: the KGB.

But when his one true love, April Rose, died at the hands of the Soviet terror machine, Bolan severed all ties with Establishment authority.

Now, after a lengthy lone-wolf struggle and much soul-searching, the Executioner has agreed to enter an "arm's-length" alliance with his government once more, reserving the right to pursue personal missions in his Everlasting War.

Prologue

Only the guilty paid for silence. After nearly two decades of searching out, recruiting or buying contacts and informants from the adversarial side, Robert Dutton knew few darker truths existed in the shadowy world of intelligence gathering. Wisdom, though, did little to calm the brewing tempest in his gut. And he suspected a storm—invisible, silent, murderous, and in the flesh—was on the way.

He cursed the static buzz in his ear, fear sweeping away the impulse to fling the cell phone across the study. Whoever was coming—and he had some notion, albeit vague, as to the identity of the opposition—had electronically severed the secured frequency to the American Embassy. The National Security Agency called it hot-wiring, their classified super-tech miniature boxes emitting laser or microwave beams through triangulation, once the source—or target operator—was identified. The interloper, however, had to be in a general proximity of fifty yards to pull off the black magic act, which told Dutton the compound had already been breached. Likewise, he found his computer screen streaked with lightning jags. He felt his guts clench with the bitter awareness that all communications to the outside world had shut down. With no chance to e-mail his wife, warn her of imminent danger, to stay put until he rounded her up.

Damn it!

Knowing there was no hope of any Marine cavalry storming the compound, he chambered a 9 mm Parabellum round into the Beretta M-9 and stowed the weapon in shoulder rigging. No, he told himself, it wasn't entirely true he was alone. His three-man team was still in the Command and Control Room, all of them armed, all of them sure to be staring at monitors jumping haywire with countertech malfeasance, alert to the sabotage. But, he wondered, was one or all three part of the plot to see he went deaf and blind? That prospect had earlier urged him to keep them in the dark, until he learned more about a possible conspiracy that could topple the administration in Washington.

Raw nerves screamed he needed to get to his wife immediately and whisk her out of Amman, a short chopper ride across the border to the relative safety of Israel where he had Mossad contacts. If he was marked as a CIA operative, he knew it stood to grim reason the opposition had most likely smoked her out as something more than a diplomatic attaché. They might kidnap her as a bargaining chip to buy his allegiance. They were compromised, no question, and that came straight from the shadow who had offered him the brown envelope only hours ago.

Briefly, he recalled the twilight encounter in the desert. He had gone there to rendezvous with an informant inside a cell of rejectionist radical Jordanians aligned with Iraqi militants. A military Humvee sat in the distance, watching the encounter, while the shadow—a Westerner brandishing an M-16—materialized out of the lengthening dusk, putting it to him to go deaf, dumb and blind, or else.

"Forget what you have learned. Take this, await further instructions…or suffer consequences."

No sale. He didn't know whether it was a setup. The Company was infamous for playing head games, separating wheat from chaff, lamb from lion, but he was a patriot, loyal to only God, country and family.

With the ultimatum now come to collect, he knew there was no point, nor time to waste shredding documents, gather the latest intel on what he'd learned from informants the past two days on what his team had tagged the "great vanishing act."

Time to fight or fly.

He marched for the double doors, briefly confounded and angry, wondering how four years of hunting down and flushing out the mystery of the weapons of mass destruction—so close but seeming like light-years away—was swirling in the bowl. The attempted bribery confirmed two critical items in his mind. First, the WMD was real, it was out there. And someone, supposedly on the side of the angels, did not want it found. The latter conclusion begged the obvious question.

Why, indeed?

He hit the door when the lights blinked out. For several moments he crouched at the barrier, heart thundering in his ears, as he silently urged the generator to kick in. Nothing. He freed the Beretta and twisted the door handle, wondering why the others were not scrambling down the hall, barreling into the study. He was out the door, weapon extended, listening to the silence, peering into the darkness in both directions down the hall when the auxiliary generator flashed on the emergency overhead lights. Heart pounding, aware he was exposed in the sudden glow, he flung himself against the wall, Beretta whipping, twelve and six. The corridor was empty, but he sensed a presence, his combat instincts torqued up, warning him the invader was close.

And the faint acrid stink bit his nose.

Ahead, he saw the pneumatic door to the Command and Control Room open. Sliding on, checking the gloomy murk to his rear, the coppery taint clawed deeper into his senses. That the door was open, however, the red light on the keypad blinking, confirmed the identity of the opposition.

Only the five men had access to the Storm Tracking Central.

Taking a deep breath, Dutton threw himself into the doorway, charged three steps in, angling hard left for the deep shadows of the corner, the Beretta sweeping the room. His stomach cramped. Peevy was slumped over his monitor, blood pooling beneath his arms, a dark ragged hole in his temple. Waters and Groome were sprawled on their backs, swivel chairs dumped on the floor. Side arms holstered, they obviously never knew what hit them. But why, he thought, should they expect to be murdered by one of their own?

Dutton shoved down his rising anger over this brutal act of treachery. He vowed to the dead they would be avenged. Danger, he knew, was part and parcel of intelligence work, but they were essentially intel brokers—Storm Trackers, tagged so because they gleaned, bought, bartered or stole information on terror operations. In short, they mapped the future of operations on both sides, predicted strike patterns, stamped flashpoints well in advance of critical mass, often war-gaming terror and counterterror scenarios on computers for Langley. They were not gunslingers, steely-eyed black ops who combed the world's hellzones for the most wanted militants, though Dutton had fired a shot in anger more than once in his day.

Retracing his path to the door, he sensed the invisible killer was nearby and closing the gap. Dead ahead, the north corridor would take him to a stairwell, which led to the subterranean garage. Trouble was, that hall bisected another corridor that circled back to his study, leaving him to wonder if the killer was laying in wait, no doubt armed with a sound-suppressed weapon.

Poised to start blasting, Dutton bolted and glimpsed the silhouette at the end of the southern hall. He saw the dark object in the killer's hand, the assassin darting for cover at the corridor's edge, then he tapped the Beretta's trigger twice on the fly. A double crack sounded, the whine of bullets ricocheting off stone in the distance, and Dutton launched himself into a full-bore sprint, the tall snake-lean figure of the killer forcing the man's name to mind like a curse word. It suddenly occurred to Dutton there could be more than one assassin under the roof, but he reached the stone door before the fear of this realization sank in. Turning the iron handle, he hauled open the massive block to the stairwell. Shooting one last look over his shoulder, he descended the narrow passageway, weapon out and ready to take down any threat as he wound his way around the first of two corners.

He hit the concrete deck running, palmed his remote box and beeped open the door locks to his GMC vehicle. Nothing unusual about the garage, as he scanned the shadows around the stone pillars, the vehicles of his dead comrades fanned out beside his ride, but there was another entrance to this underground lot, and he was sure the assassin knew of its existence. Certain he heard the faint scuffle of feet over stone toward the north exit, he flung open the door, jumped behind the wheel, scanning the garage. Determined he would shoot or bulldoze his exit out of there, he was keying the ignition when he spotted the inert figure on the shotgun seat in the corner of his eye. He was cursing himself for what might prove a fatal oversight, gun up and tracking, when he turned and faced the unmoving shape.

And felt his blood freeze.

"Oh, God, oh, God, no…"

He heard his cry trail off, feeble and distant, as he felt his heart jackhammer, believing for a moment fear and adrenaline had warped his senses, rendering the world an hallucination, spinning in his eyes, off its axis. The sound volumed into a pure bellow of animal rage, as he reached over, ready to shake her, call her name. But he had seen dead bodies, before and the blank stare and dark hole in her temple confirmed the murderous deed.

The impulse dropped over him like a wall of stone, his hand reaching for the door, ready now to fight or die, if only in the name of vengeance. But Dutton discovered he was grabbing air. The head butt shot out of nowhere. He felt his nose mashed into his face, caught his howl of agony vanishing somewhere in the blast furnace of scalding knives tearing through his brain, then number two hammer slammed him off the eyebrow. As blood stung his eyes, blinding him, he was vaguely aware of hands clawing into his shoulders like talons.

Suddenly, he was aware his own hands were empty, bell rung, reflexes for anything resembling a counterattack nearly frozen by pain. He was airborne next, wrenched from the seat, swiping at the blood in his eyes when the bastard teed off with a kick to his groin. Another grenade of white-hot pain exploded, scalp to toes, dropping him to his knees. Paralyzed, he tasted bile and blood on his lips, and strained to make out the assassin through the burning mist in his eyes.

"All you had to do was take the money and follow a few simple directions. It could have been so easy. But here we are. Me, disappointed in my fellow man. You, sucking on a final few moments of rage and grief and disillusionment."

Dutton coughed, sucked wind, determined then not to give the bastard the satisfaction of seeing him begging for his life. Yes, he thought, here we are. He found it all so incredible; it struck him as the deluded fantasy of psychopaths. Or was there more to it? What? Greed? Power? Delusions of grandeur? He stared up at the assassin who took a step back, the Beretta held low by his side.

"What in God's name have you done, Locklin?" Dutton asked plainly.

"Beyond luring your wife out of the embassy under the

pretense of an emergency—the emergency being you—I haven't done anything in God's name."

Dutton spit blood, surprised how the powerful hatred he felt toward the killer dulled the edge of physical torment. "You rotten bastard…she didn't know anything."

"She's CIA, Dutton. She would have figured it out on her own, or you would have told her one night over some pillow talk."

"What you're doing…it will never happen."

"Wrong, friend, it's already happening, but what you think you found out is just a small part of the big picture. And, by the way, maybe you're thinking the Company station chief here in Jordan will make this up to you, stabilize the situation already in play, sound the alarm from Langley to the Pentagon? Who do you think put me in charge of security at the embassy and to monitor you and your Storm Trackers? The official paper trail that put my seal of approval in your face is so back-channeled and convoluted it would take an act of God to trace it to the original source. Besides, the good CSC has already gone the way of your wife."

Dutton felt adrenaline drive away the sludge in his limbs, fisted some of the blood out of his eyes, glanced to the open door and spotted his weapon on the seat. He didn't think he'd make the four-foot lunge, but he had to try. If he kept the traitor talking while the cobwebs cleared, he might be able to pull off a lightning retaliatory strike.

"Okay, I give up. You sound like you're in a talking mood, Locklin, so why not tell me why you've become a dirty rat bastard selling out to the enemy?"

Locklin laughed. "There is no enemy, Dutton—other than the people you think you pledge allegiance to."

"I work for the United States government, Locklin."

"So do I. Listen up, here's a lesson on the facts of life. I'm sure you've heard how the victors in any war write history, how the winners determine who the bad guys are, how those on the winning side can tell future generations how they wore the armor of righteousness and made the world a better place."

"That's what this is about? Winning? Writing history?"

"Not writing it—creating it, making the future happen. You're a Storm Tracker, Dutton. You know something about predicting the future, how to look into the eyes of tomorrow's incubating conflicts and figure out how it will turn out, more or less. All the future is, well, it's just an extension of the past. Men making the same mistakes. I'm just an instrument of the future and the people you so naively pledged allegiance to— the CIA, your informants, hell, maybe even the President of the United States—they're not going to be a part of the coming future."

The more his vision cleared, the more sickened Dutton felt at the face of pure evil looming over him. He knew he would never leave the garage breathing, the veil of darkness shadowing Locklin's face warning him the killer's blustering stance was over. The Beretta was rising.

It was over.

Dutton launched himself off the ground, hand streaking out for his weapon. He braced himself for the bullets to start tearing into him. It was either a miracle of speed and brazenness on his part or Locklin simply toying with him, but he had the Beretta in hand, heart pumping with lethal intent. Dutton wheeled, instinct shouting he wouldn't make it. But a distant faint voice in his head told him that someone, somewhere would stand up to this monstrous evil before it unleashed its abomination on the world. At near point-blank range, he felt the cracking thunder lance his eardrums, a nanosecond before the 9 mm hammer drilled his forehead and doused the lights.

1

The blinding light usually broke them before he came in to close the game. Of course, he thought, there was prep work before the hardball questions were fired off, something extra for Task Force Talon's time and trouble having to hunt some of them down in the first place. Plus, getting it straight up front, their will would be little more than wet dung to be molded in his hands. For instance, the detainee—or, in the private parlance of interrogators, the chum or the contaminants—seemed to always come to him requiring warm up where it hurt most—on the mug. A shot or two to the nose, squelching beak to crimson mash potatoes while pinballing those firewheels through the brain, was a decent jump start to poke a chink in defiant armor. It let them know right off whatever they'd heard about the Geneva Convention was simply the whiny nonsense of Western journalists who couldn't fathom the real world. Naturally, before the festivities started, they were stripped naked, strapped to the cold steel chair, humiliation hard at work right away to rob the chum of any pride. He let them stew for, say, anywhere from thirty-six to forty-eight hours like that, no food or water, no sleep.

Alone, seething, shamed and frightened, pinned by the light.

The problem was, the white light could break a man down

to a gibbering idiot. No longer, then, did he leave them with eyelids forced open by clamps. He needed hard intel from lucid tongues, not raving lunatics fit only for a straitjacket. Consider the murdering rabble he had to deal with and break, though, he figured it was forgiveable if they lost one or two along the way, learning from their own mistakes how far to push it as they went.

The rock music and the air conditioner mounted on the white wall were the newest additions, both of them personal touches. Piped in at jumbojet decibels, the guard monitoring the 8x10 cell—the Conversion Room it was called—had the discretion to decide how long to blast the detainee with screeching guitar riffs and primal drumbeats. He could grant the prisoner whatever period of blessed silence he chose before blaring back the same godawful song. With the transfer complete, the worst of the worst militants from Guantanamo Bay found themselves in a remote jungle hellhole. Smack on the Brazil-Paraguay-Argentina border, few human beings knew it existed and even fewer wanted to know.

It was his show.

Zipping up the bomber jacket, he pulled the door shut behind him, then slipped on the leather gloves. Even with the black sunglasses he squinted, taking a few moments to adjust to the white glare. Two steps across the polyethylene tarp, the plastic crinkling beneath rubber-soled combat boots, and he saw the detainee flinch at the sound. Good, he thought, no permanent ear damage. If possible, he liked to keep his style of interrogation more low key, direct, friendly even, unlike the shouting and barking his two comrades enjoyed.

He took a moment to inspect the damage his starter and middle relief had inflicted earlier, stepping into the halo, shielding the battered face with his shadow. The swollen eyelids fluttered open as best they could, then cracked to slits, the detainee groaning, shivering so hard in the restraints around his arms and legs it made him wonder if the bolts would hold down the chair. They'd done quite the hit parade on the ribs, he saw, both sides a quilt work pattern, layered in black and purple. And the strained wheezing told him every breath the Iraqi drew was like taking a hot knife through the torso.

He fired up a cigarette, inhaled a healthy lungful through it and blew the cloud in the prisoner's face, meshing smoke with pluming breath. Though he had his closing mentally scripted he still wondered where to start. Whether Kharballah al-Tikriti was the bastard son of the Burrowed Bearded Rat—as rumor indicated—was of minor importance, as long as that knowledge remained a secret shared only by those closest to him.

"I am Colonel James Braden, commander of Task Force Talon," he began, the detainee gagging and wincing as he shrouded him with another wave of smoke. "I am what is called a closer, but from where you sit, Kharballah, I am the alpha and the omega, I am the only friend in the world you have at this moment. I stand between you and death."

He thought he spotted the residue of defiant life still in the eyes, maybe a spark of hatred. Sliding to the side, blowing smoke, he watched al-Tikriti shut his eyes, then the Iraqi cut loose a stream of profanity mixing Arabic with English. Braden was more amazed than angry. None of the others had made it this far, but al-Tikriti was still going strong.

"That is the only answer you will get from me," the prisoner said finally.

"Have it your way, by all means." Braden freed the pliers from his coat pocket, clamped them on the Iraqi's smashed nose, twisted. "Maybe I didn't tell you, but I understand Arabic, Kharballah," he growled in the prisoner's native tongue, as al-Tikriti howled and fresh blood burst from the pulped beak.

"Let's try this again," the American said, switching to English, releasing the pincers and stepping back as blood spattered on plastic. Braden began his slow shark circle around the prisoner. "What I'm looking for, Kharballah, is the golden tip that will lead me to the Holy Grail—the rest of what you and the others were smuggling into Turkey when you were picked up. How about it? Where's the rest of it?"

"What you took was all I know of."

Braden snapped the pliers. The lie he read in al-Tikriti's eyes was swept away by fear. "That's not what your fellow holy warriors told me. Yeah, Kharballah, they talked."

"Then what do you need me for?" the prisoner responded.

"Before I get into all that, let me explain the facts of life as I know them. I am in personal possession of satellite imagery that details a lot of truck traffic. Hell, for a while there we tracked whole convoys of eighteen-wheelers all over the map. We've got Damascus, through Kirkuk, Tikrit to Damascus, they're coming from Tehran even, all these eighteen-wheelers, SUVs, transport trucks heading straight for the Turk border. I'm thinking maybe we Americans ought to just build a few superfreeways while we're putting your country back on its feet." It was an exaggeration, but al-Tikriti didn't know what Braden knew.

"Trouble is, satellites have a tough time seeing things through the clouds. We know you had contacts in the Kurd-controlled far east of Turkey, but we doubt you were doing business with a people the former regime wanted to gas to extinction. So, I'm thinking you found a spot to stash all or a large chunk of it, but you had help from militant Turks. How do I know they're Turks, you ask? I can't be positive, but you people often forget we have ways to intercept conversations over what you believe are secured lines. Then there's e-mail, faxes, Internet chat rooms. We get hold of your computers.

You think you've deleted your files, but we have guys who can bring up these things called ghosts on the hard drive."

"I know what you can do."

Braden smiled. "The wonders of technology. Maybe you see where I'm headed with this."

"How can I tell you what I do not know? I was simply what you might call a foot soldier."

Braden put an edge to his voice. "That's not the way Abdullah and Dajul told it."

"Then they lied to you."

"I cut them a deal, Kharballah, the same one you can have. Hell, you put me on the scent, I might even give you back some of that five hundred thousand I relieved you of. Now, I need to know whatever rendezvous points you had in Turkey. I need to know the approximate numbers—a rough guess will do—and specifically what the ordnance is. And I need to know where it's all squirreled away. Real simple equation here. Names, numbers and how to get hold of who you were off-loading the ordnance to. Talk and you walk to fight another day."

"I know nothing," al-Tikriti said.

Braden lit another smoke off his dying butt and bobbed his head at the detainee. Time to hit him in the pride, he decided. "Doesn't it bother you, Kharballah?"

"Does what bother me?"

"How you gave up without a fight, left the dying to your brothers in jihad." Braden saw he'd scored, figured the prisoner was still steaming at the memory of hacking on tear gas, stumbling around in the smoke, hurling his weapon away, hands up.

"We had you figured for a lion sure to go out with a roar. Instead you whimpered, not one shot fired. Hell, I thought you were going to start crying like some old hag, the way I recall it. Threw away your AK so fast—"

"You surprised me. You gassed us."

"That's what separates the men from the boys and the bullies in a fight, Kharballah. Being able to adjust, take a few on the chin, but dig in and charge back, swinging. That's the way of the warrior, Kharballah. He fights, even when the odds are stacked against him. He goes all the way, even if he's looking at Goliath." Braden smothered the scowl with a smoke cloud.

"That's right, honey, I'm calling you a coward. You scumbags run around, trying to make everybody think you're mean as the day is long, that you're willing to die for your twisted holy war. But the first sign somebody's ready to fight back and wax your ass you cut and run. A few car bombs, killing unarmed women and children, sweetheart, hardly proves you have the biggest pair on the block." Braden paused to let al-Tikriti eat his shame.

"I want to know about Khirbul, and don't tell me it's a Kurd stronghold the Iranians run heroin through. Well, sweetheart, I'm waiting."

"And so you shall keep waiting. You can leave me here for a week, a month like this, I will tell you nothing."

Braden's gut told him that was the only truth he would get out of al-Tikriti. He tossed the pliers, dropped the cigarette and ground it out on the plastic, then unzipped his jacket, displaying the shouldered Beretta. There were still other warm bodies to work with. "That your final answer?"

The Iraqi chuckled. "What? You beat me, now you're going to shoot me?"

"You don't believe I will?"

"You're an American. I am a prisoner of war. There's such a thing, I believe, called the rights of prisoners as established by the Geneva Convention," al-Tikriti stated.

Braden unleathered the Beretta, drew a bead between al-Tikriti's widening eyes and showed him just what he thought about the Geneva Convention.

2

John Brolinsky was worried about his job and reputation, wondering if he was being set up for public scandal and ridicule. Stranger—and worse—duplicity had happened over the years at the NSA. Those sharks on the man-eating end of the food chain were always looking for fresh guilty meat. If a man wasn't as clean as a newborn, the conventional wisdom held he was ripe for blackmail—a definite liability when it came to guarding secrets or protecting national security.

Without question, a gentleman's club—the gentleman part the grossest of misnomers from where he sat—was the most unlikely and unprofessional of places to rendezvous with one of the most powerful men in the White House. But here he was, nursing a club soda that was dropped off without his ordering the drink. He claimed the deep back booth the man had told him would be empty. Just wait, the man had told him, relax, enjoy the ambience.

As if I could, even if I was so inclined, the NSA man thought.

Given what he'd learned and suspected was at stake, he decided he had no choice but to ride out this tawdry scenario, take his chances and hope the walls of his own world wouldn't crash down.

There had been directions into Washington, then down into the underground parking garage, Brolinsky wondering the whole drive in from Fort Meade if he was being followed. Rush hour waning to bring on the dinner crowd, he'd noticed the garage bowels were nearly empty. The attendant presented him a pass, no money up front. The same deal transpired at the club, he recalled. The bartender indicated his booth on the way in, waitresses and dancers steering clear of the table, as if they were on standing orders not to disturb.

Simply put, it felt wrong.

No black op warring against the shadows of evil in the world, he was grateful nonetheless he'd brought the Beretta 92-F from his think tank, shouldered now beneath his suit jacket.

He glanced around, avoiding anything other than a passing scan at the collective object of desire onstage. It was a mixed pack of hyenas, blue and white collar, probably a few crack hoodlums on the prowl. No one made eye contact with him, and that was the only plus he could find. Problem was, if the bartender had a clue as to his identity…

He was a church-going family man with a wife and two teenaged daughters. He would be forced into retirement, disgraced, even divorce could be in the cards if the situation took a bad turn.

He spotted the man in glasses and a dark cashmere coat descending the short flight of steps, recognizable enough after two recent stints on the Sunday morning talking head circuit. Sizing him up, Brolinsky found it hard to believe the man had the President's ear, one of three "invisibles" who had personally engineered the unofficial Special Countermeasure Task Force. An aide to two former officials so high up the chain at the NSA, and now part of the President's inner circle—rumor had it their word on worldwide intelligence operations could have been carved in stone—and Michael Rubin struck him as nondescript. He had a bald shiny pate, thick eyewear and a face so scrubbed it glistened for a moment as he passed through the stage lights. Brolinsky suddenly thought of him as the Pink Man.

"You look distressed. You don't like my choice of meeting places?" Rubin said in greeting.

Brolinsky watched as the Pink Man claimed a seat, slid closer to him in the booth. There was something in the small dark eyes he didn't trust, but couldn't decide what exactly. Arrogance? Deceit and treachery forged on the anvil of jealous guarding of national secrets? Or was he reaching to find a dark side, gather up his own ammo to use against the man's character in the event his own might be assassinated?

"There's a lot to be distressed about these days," he told the Pink Man.

"So it seems."

"You come here often?" he asked, thinking Rubin looked more the type to get his voyeur kicks off the Internet.

The Pink Man smiled. "Is this where I'm supposed to check you for a wire? Not that it would matter, since we both know our people can make a minimike or recorder look like a simple quarter or belt buckle."

"You want to frisk me like some common criminal? Makes me wonder what's to hide," Brolinsky said.

"Your tone and look tell me you seem to think there is. The tipoff, however, was your three attempted calls to reach someone besides a flunky in the National Security Council the past few hours—as in an urgent message for the national security adviser. You should have contacted our people at the White House first, that would have been the prudent course of action in these 'times of distress.'"

"By your people, you mean Durham or Griswald."

"That would have been the more professional route."

"I'm not one of you."

Rubin ignored the remark, said, "The Man just ripped everyone within earshot a new one. Intelligence operatives are being burned by this country's worst enemies, as I'm sure you know, the belief being these leaks are coming straight from key upper-echelon White House staff."

"They are," Brolinsky stated flatly.

"Do tell. Then my assumption about you was correct. Very well. Whatever it is you're trying to tell me—and I think I know where you're headed—I wouldn't make too much noise about what's happened overseas. I'm sure you can understand the delicate political nature such recent mishaps could create."

"You want to keep it from the press."

"The President wants to, no, he needs to keep it under the White House roof. There's a larger situation at stake."

"Really?" Brolinsky scanned the crowd, finding it hard to believe they were ready to launch full-bore into a chat about national security in such a public dump, then figured between the grinding rock and roll and the howling banshees anything short of a shouting match might be safe.

"We have complete privacy, I assure you," Rubin stated. "Feel free to lay out this urgency of yours."

"There are occasions I am required to report directly, in person, to either the President or the national security adviser."

"I'm aware of that. As I'm aware you're aware of who I am."

"Then I assume you've heard about Amman."

"The CIA Storm Tracking Station. Four operators and the team leader's wife found shot dead. Lured from the embassy over what appears to have been a fabricated emergency regarding her husband."

"Bad news travels fast."

The Pink Man sighed. "Your point?"

"We're looking at dead bodies of American intelligence operatives turning up all over the map—two incidents—or mishaps, as you put it—happening in less than a week."

"You're referring to Turkey."

Brolinsky grunted. "Throw in two NSA and a CIA operative gunned down, same MO in Istanbul and Ankara, apparently—though nothing about him seems verifiable—the same military attaché who headed embassy security in Turkey vanishing off the face of the earth after both incidents. Well, it doesn't take much to see a pattern emerging."

Rubin chuckled. "So, you're running around, armed with conspiracy theories, itching to tell senior White House officials, or the President himself, the sky is falling."

"It's beginning to shake out as more than a theory. He calls himself Locklin, but no one seems to know who he works for. You know the type, buried so deep off-the-books the man doesn't even have a Social Security number. A freelancer owned and armed by various intelligence agencies to do the really dirty work. The ultimate deniable expendable. A little digging, a fact here, an educated guess there, a few matters are becoming clearer to me by the hour."

Rubin laid on a patronizing tone. "Please, don't waste my time with rumor and speculation. Please, tell me you have real hard intelligence to back you up—or I walk."

"Contacts in and beyond the normal channels. Plus, maybe you've heard, we're in the great new age of sharing information, mutual cooperation and so forth between various alphabet soup agencies. The gist of it, I'm being told the same ghost story where this Locklin is concerned."

"Perhaps whatever you heard is just a story."

"I suspect someone with major league clout, real close to the President, managed to land what amounts to little more than an assassin in the laps of both embassies to smoke out these operatives."

"To what purpose?" Rubin asked.

Brolinsky paused, wondering how much he should tell this former NSA official. He decided to forge ahead. If he got the

Pink Man talking, agitated, boxed him in a corner there was a chance to catch him a lie. And if that happened it would put him one step closer to confirming the bombshell of a dark nagging suspicion.

"Kill the messengers about to hurl open Pandora's box. Some or all of whom either knew or were on the scent of that banned ordnance with delivery systems that left the country in question right before the Shock and Awe began," he told Rubin. "A lot of nasty stuff, which, had it been buried in the sand or dumped in the Tigris or Euphrates, we would have known about it by now, since the general consensus among the science community is an ecological and environmental Bhopal meets Chernobyl would have swept the country in question, an invisible firestorm that might have struck down or driven out the Coalition forces."

Rubin shook his head. "I'm not tracking how you equate this supposed Houdini act with recent events." He glanced at his watch. "Kindly and quickly enlighten me."

"Colonel James Braden, United States Special Forces, ran a black ops unit in Afghanistan. Fact—he lost five ops in an ambush by Taliban and al Qaeda fighters near the Afghan-Pakistani border. Nonconventional weapons were used in the fight, specifically VX. The way I heard it, he was one step behind netting the twenty-five-foot Saudi shark. Rumor—he liked the hands-on approach when interrogating prisoners. A few people in the loop privately confirmed his tactical techniques for Q and A, then later changed their story, all of whom shortly after disappeared. Instead of getting court-martialed and landing in prison for life the man damn near received a presidential citation. He was put in charge of Task Force Talon. Handpicked his own troops."

He paused as the dancer finished her number to lukewarm applause, scanned faces for a sign of special interest aimed his way.

"I'm listening," Rubin said, clearly getting impatient.

"Locklin's description matches an operative, believed seen with Braden in Kurd-controlled Turkey right before a convoy suspected of hauling the last of the wicked stuff was hit by Braden, his Task Force Talon and Turk Special Forces. Rumor—Locklin was Braden's inside eyes and ears to the mystery of the vanished ordnance. Suspicion—the Iraqis had help from our side smuggling the nasty stuff out of the country. Why? If I could raise the Storm Trackers from the dead I might find out. The word I get is that whatever they were smuggling into Turkey was there at the time of the hit, but is now nowhere to be found. Which leads me to Camp Triangle. I'm sure you've heard of it?"

"You would be wise to keep all of this to yourself," Rubin said.

"Is that a threat?"

"Merely a suggestion."

"In that case, stick your advice." The scowl told him he'd struck a nerve, sure now the Pink Man had something to hide. He decided to torque up the heat and attitude.

"I know a chosen group of the worst of militants detained at Guantanamo Bay were rounded up in the dead of night and whisked off in a C-130 to this corner of Brazil that meets Paraguay and Argentina. It was a secret pact arranged by the White House in collusion with Brazil to let Camp Triangle come to life in this neck of jungle. I'm thinking to keep the natives with the big guns and the power down there quiet and cooperative, Congress passes a massive foreign aid package to Brazil, ostensibly to help the Brazilians combat crime, corruption, poverty—but I think both of us suspect into whose coffers all those billions will disappear.

"Now, I think the President was convinced by your buddies in the Special Countermeasure Task Force that the Triangle—a haven for drug and arms smugglers, international crime cartels, Hamas, al Qaeda and other Arab terror groups paying for safe refuge while planning operations—is a treasure trove of invaluable intelligence. That much truth they spoke. Word is, however, the Man was further swayed by reasons laid out to him about the basic necessity to spread the growing problem of housing captured fanatics in another but classified direction. Seems Task Force Talon was rounding up militants quicker than there was space at Gitmo to hold them. My sources inform me that some of the detainees removed from Gitmo—calling themselves the Warrior Sons of Islam—claim direct blood lines to some of the world's most wanted terrorists, including a couple of household names.

"Now, a young Marine, rotated out of your classified detainee base, was en route to tell a very interesting story to the Justice Department about what's going on down there in Camp Triangle, only he turned up dead in his vehicle, the victim of an apparent self-inflicted gunshot wound to the head."

Rubin didn't blink. "And all of this related to White House leaks, how and why?"

"There's more, unless you're in a big rush to race out of here."

Rubin gestured with his hand for Brolinsky to continue.

"Wolfe-Binder."

"Never heard of it."

He suspected Rubin was lying, but Brolinsky didn't miss a beat. He pressed on. "There are twenty-seven industrial chemical plants in the continental United States. Seven which manufacture defensive biochem weapons—a definite misnomer—but this is what we tell the Russians to make it look like we're honoring the treaty to ban biochem weapons. Number eight plant, Wolfe-Binder, just popped up on the radar screen. This classified plant in New Orleans is purported to be an armed camp, guys in HAZMAT suits, clandestine flights leaving in the middle of the night, loaded down with more, I suspect, than just agricultural pesticide, though that's the claim as to what they're processing. I'm sure you know insecticide is a main precursor for nerve gas."

"Among nonflammable retardants and other precursors, but I don't have the recipe at my fingertips," Rubin said, sounding bored.

Brolinsky ignored the brush-off. "How do I know all this about Wolfe-Binder, you ask? The plant's assistant manager became suspicious when men in black fatigues wouldn't allow a manifest or any record of these midnight runs to be recorded. So he does his civic duty, puts in a call to the FBI. FBI and Justice Department agents go down there to take a look, but the whistle-blower has disappeared. The story they get is the man was a drunk, had a habit of disappearing for days, or calling in sick. Utter bullshit, since anyone with common sense would have fired him in the first place." Brolinsky paused, saw the Pink Man's dark eyes flicker.

"Never mind I think the guy was dumped in the bayou as gator bait, the plant was a one-eighty picture of what the FBI was told. No armed guards. No spacesuits. Every drum and vat that was tested turned out to be pesticide and other industrial chemicals. Spotless as a saint. However, most of the manifests indicated the bulk of the pesticide was being flown to Brasilia. When questioned, the manager claimed it had something to do with the recent foreign aid package to Brazil that Congress passed."

"Once more…"

"Your Special Countermeasure Task Force is an off-the-record supersecret service for the President. Which puts them, in my opinion, too close to the President, with too much power and authority in the White House," Brolinsky said.

"They—we—are more than that."

"Right. You plan foreign itineraries, map out logistics for

overseas jaunts, specifically Mideast countries, you handle threats to the President directly. You handle foreign agendas for the VP, diplomats, cabinet members, supposedly plugging up security holes against assassinations, suicide bombers and such." Brolinsky smiled, shook his head.

"How did you do it? How did you manage to get the President to approve of what is essentially an unofficial secret government enforcement, maybe even a black ops arm right inside the White House? I can only imagine the bitter rivalries it's created. The Secret Service for one thing, taking a back seat, step and fetch it for you people. I can only picture the scandal that would threaten to topple the administration if news of this reached the public."

"Not your concern. What is your point with all this conspiracy conjecture?"

Brolinsky looked Rubin dead in the eye. "I can't prove it, not yet, but I suspect the leaks came from someone in the SCTF."

There was a pause, then Rubin said, "Are you done?"

"You have the floor."

"We know where the leaks were coming from. If I tell you—"

"You'll have to shoot me?"

"Nothing quite so melodramatic."

Why wasn't he so sure about that? Brolinsky wondered. He tensed as Rubin's hand disappeared beneath the table. The Pink Man dug into his coat pocket, then flipped three one-hundred-dollar bills on the table. Tribute for the bartender's accommodation confirmed, Brolinsky figured the parking garage attendant was treated to the same favor. What the hell was going on?

Rubin slid out of the booth. "Let's finish this talk in your vehicle. Unless you don't think you can handle the truth. In that case, stay and enjoy the show."

Brolinsky hesitated, watching as Rubin walked away, then rose to follow. He fixed his stare on Rubin's back, warning bells clanging in his head as he climbed the steps. Suddenly the Pink Man didn't want to talk in public? In his profession, paranoia did not destroy, he thought, as he cut the gap, out the door, falling in lockstep beside the Pink Man as they navigated their course through the sparse sidewalk crowd. He was tempted to look over his shoulder, check every passing face for any sign of a threat, but didn't want to tip Rubin he was on edge, ready to go for broke.

"Perhaps I state the obvious, but we live in very strange, dangerous and volatile times, my friend," Rubin said, rounding the corner, picking up his march a notch as they closed on the garage.

"The worst, however, is on the horizon. And my task force knows this for a fact. We have garnered the complete trust of the President because we have delivered intelligence that has saved untold innocent lives, even prevented a third world war. Like the late Storm Trackers, we search out and predict the future, know what the opposition is going to do before they do. For example, take Pakistan. Say militants or sympathizers in the military take—or seize—control of the country, armed thus with the keys and access codes to their nuclear arsenal. Meaning they have the ultimate suicide bomber in charge. Could it happen? Well, my friend, we brought intelligence to the Oval Office that had already thwarted just such a palace coup, but who is to say there won't be another attempt? So, you see, certain, uh, extreme measures were necessary in order to insure that the President stays breathing and the world remains safe from nuclear blackmail.

"The Man, for your information, sees us as his personal intelligence gurus, what some tabloid press hound, were one to catch a whiff, might call necromancers, seers. Bottom line, we deliver the goods. The Man took note of our astonishing successes where others could not perform. It took some long hours, brainstorming about the creation of SCTF, but he gave the nod."

Brolinsky saw the attendant was gone as they hit the mouth of the garage. The gate was down on both sides. Rubin crouched and slipped to the other side. Brolinsky did the same, the Pink Man informing him the pass he received earlier would let him out.

In silence, Brolinsky strained his ears for any sound that might alert him to a waiting presence, as he descended beside Rubin into the gloomy bowels. Feeling the hackles rise on the back of his neck, he spotted his SUV, parked against the far wall, no other vehicles in sight.

"His name was Jason Lind," Rubin suddenly said. "His official title was chief deputy of counter intelligence. CIA. He was always present at the President's daily national security briefs. Turns out he had a nasty little hobby involving Internet porn, creating his own lurid Websites—I'll skip the particulars. Anyway, he was found in his home about an hour ago. Self-inflicted gunshot wound to the head, a suicide note stating he was behind the leaks. It's been verified."

How convenient, Brolinsky thought, there seemed to be an epidemic of suicide lately by those who counted the most, taking any dark truths with them to the beyond.

"There you have it," Rubin said.

Sensing a presence lurking in the garage, thinking he spotted a shadow darting behind a pillar to his nine, Brolinsky began scouring his flanks, then glimpsed Rubin tug on a pair of black gloves. His heart was racing to meteoric levels.

And then it happened.

The Glock .45 looked almost comical in the Pink Man's hand, but the dark eyes, alive with murderous intent, froze Brolinsky. In the next instant he recognized the bittersweet quasi-gasoline stink swarming his nose, but the arm was locked around his neck, the rag smothering his face before he could react. It was strange, he thought, the fumes swelling his brain, the lights fading. The Marine, the plant whistle-blower and Jason Lind flashed through his mind. He found himself wishing he could tell the Pink Man somehow, some way the last bitter laugh would land on his head. He had contacted a former mission controller at the NSA and clued her in to his suspicions. That hopeful thought trailed to a fading anger and sorrow that he would never again see his family as he succumbed to warm swaddling blackness.

3

Major Alan Hawke, United States Special Forces, had heard the rumors, but seeing was, indeed, believing. What was inside the hovel, under medical examination, added a new and nervous wrinkle to the mission. It was just the kind of horror—and hassle—he didn't need. This wasn't Task Force Talon of Afghanistan infamy, where he had served under Colonel Braden, and soldiers turned a blind eye, or else. Out here, there were new grunts on the block who might go over his head, flap tongues to starred brass who would land his neck on a chopping block. At that moment, he wrestled with any number of conflicting loyalties as to whom to report to, aware his next move could well lead to a court-martial. But he knew what had to be done.

And he knew he would do it, if he wanted to survive, if he didn't want his own atrocities brought to light.

Listening to the whapping blades of his Apache helicopter, the two Hueys framing the stone hovel in a white halo from a hundred yards south over his shoulder, feeling the swirling grit sting his neck, he silently urged Task Force Iron Hawk's medic to emerge with a final report. Feeling the ghosts of fifteen dead Iraqis, he scoured the black walls of the wadi, M-16/M-203 combo ready to cut loose at any rebel who might have fled the firefight some eight hours earlier.

It had been a fluke, stumbling across the building while

roving the skies in search of armed runners. Going through
the door, ready to shoot, they found the two victims, stricken
and stretched out on prayer rugs from God only knew what,
though he had his suspicions. A man and a woman, husband
and wife, it turned out. His interpreter, donning a HAZMAT
suit, had pried from them a very unnerving tale.

And confirmed what he'd been hearing during the briefs
the past several months.

He told himself he really had no business this far north,
edged up against the Turk border, this neck of rugged mountain country. Kurd-controlled, there was enough ethnic hatred wandering around to mow down any resistance rabble
who escaped their steel talons. But his orders didn't always
come direct from Central Command.

The problem was how to avoid reporting what he'd found.

He saw the spacesuit emerge through the doorway, Captain Medley removing his helmet. With no way to read the
grim expression, Hawke waited until the man was on top of
him.

Medley appeared to gather his thoughts on how to proceed. "The good news is it doesn't appear to be a bio agent,
but I'd like to draw blood, take tissue samples for further examination," he said.

"No."

Medley looked aghast. "But, sir—"

"What's killing them?" Hawke asked.

"Killed."

Hawke groaned to himself, more an act than anything
else, hoping Medley read the noise as disappointment at the
lack of information. In this case ignorance was bliss.

Medley continued. "The spasms, the manner in which
their limbs locked up, asphyxiation, all classic symptoms of
exposure to a nerve agent."

"Sergeant Ellis informed me they had just returned from

across the Turk border, delivering some cargo they could or would not specify."

"My guess is they handled the agent, a seal broke on a drum, or whatever they were shipping it in. They must have been exposed to high doses given their symptoms."

"Are you telling me this wasn't their first trip?"

"That, running the nerve agent in faulty containers, or there's a good chance they overturned the vehicle, dumped the cargo, got splashed in the process. For a nerve agent, inhalation or direct skin contact will do the deed."

"If your scenario is correct, they should have dropped right then, across the border."

"Not necessarily. It would depend on how much of the agent they were exposed to. Either way, they're long past any atropine injection now."

Hawke looked his medic dead in the eye. "You are to forget what you saw here. Do you copy, Captain?" He could see Medley didn't like it, was poised to argue, but seemed to think better of it.

"Yes, sir," the medic said with reluctance.

"Hop on board then," he told Medley, then whistled at the four shadows hunkered in the wadi, rotating his raised fist.

So it was true, he thought, holding his ground, waiting while his troops hustled past him to board the Hueys. Whatever had begun in Afghanistan, all the talk he'd heard from CIA spooks dancing with the devil, Braden…

Marching for his grounded Hueys, forging into the whirlwind, Hawke raised his Apache crew and ordered, "Give me one right down Broadway, mister."

The order copied, he gathered speed. The Hellfire missile flamed away from its pod. As the thunder pealed behind, and suspecting how the sins of the past were about to create hell on earth, he thought, God help us. God help us all.

4

"Calm down."

"That's a Presidential Directive, in case you've never seen one, Colonel. And in case you haven't guessed yet, we've got an official human shitstorm headed this way. I, for one, can say I don't much care for the tone from the Oval Office. It damn near hints at treason."

Examining the faxed letter with the presidential seal in the Humvee's headlights, Colonel Braden glanced at General Compton, bared his teeth at the beefy tub in jungle fatigues, then returned to reading their orders.

"Someone talked, Colonel, maybe even someone we thought we could trust. Which, if true, means they know what you've been doing down here!"

The more Compton whined, worried, no doubt, about saving his own fatass, the more Braden felt the blood pressure pulsing in his eardrums. He imagined he heard the HK-33 assault rifle slung over his shoulder calling the general's name. From behind him he heard the splash, witnessed the sight of al-Tikriti's body, wrapped in a plastic shroud, being dumped in the river by two of Task Force Talon's finest. It interrupted the man's bleating for all of two seconds.

"Maybe you want to tell me how we're going to account for two murdered detainees. Maybe you've got a makeup kit

I don't know about that we can use to patch up and mask four more who look like they've gone a few rounds with—"

"Calm down!" Braden shouted.

Braden's hands shook with simmering rage. He scanned the next two lines, but Compton was nearly barking in his ear.

"You listening to me? We are looking at a fat whopping mess that no amount of sterilizing will sanitize unless we burn the whole damn camp down and build it back from scratch. I have cargo back at camp with no manifests, no serial numbers. I have the Brazilian making noise to return to Brasilia and blow the whistle unless he sees—"

"Calm the fuck down! Let me think here!" Braden was seething.

Whether it was the feral look he turned on Compton or that they both knew he was actually the one on the hot seat with blood on his hands, the General shut his mouth. Braden turned his back to Compton, took a moment to survey the walls of lush vegetation flanking the dirt trail, and composed his thoughts. It was one of the last stretches of jungle in this remote outpost, a few miles east of Camp Triangle, where they could dispose of their mistakes. There was a time, he believed, when caimans and ferocious little fish with razor-teeth would have devoured decomposing flesh.

The problem was the new massive hydroelectric generating plant. He hoped the bodies didn't bob to the surface if they made it to the dam's wall. That would prove another, perhaps fatal mistake, since it appeared Washington thought it smelled the putrefaction. Listening to the caw and screech of wild birds in the distant veil of black, feeling his nerves soothed by the chitter of insects, he bobbed his head and turned to face Compton.

Braden wadded up the Presidential Directive and tossed it into the brush. "Okay, General, here's what we do before we greet with open arms and winning smiles this asshole colonel from Washington—"

5

Dead men could talk by the manner in which they died.

He might be thinking in cop terms, more or less, violent death hardly something new in his profession, but Mack Bolan couldn't help but feel the ghosts of slain American intelligence operatives—a young Marine and a missing civilian who had sounded an SOS to the FBI. The Executioner surveyed the industrial chemical plant from a wooded knoll, his surveillance post roughly forty yards due north of Gate One.

What, exactly, the dead had to do with Wolfe-Binder Chemicals along the Mississippi River he didn't know. But eight bodies, that he knew of, were already attached to what he believed were several mysteries. He had never talked to the victims before they were murdered—or allegedly committed suicide—but the pieces of a sordid puzzle had been coming together for close to a week. And the mystery darkened with each passing hour.

Several situations begging large nasty questions had been brought to Bolan's attention by Hal Brognola. His longtime friend was a high-ranking official at the Justice Department, but that was just the public face. In the shadow world of covert ops, Brognola oversaw Stony Man Farm, the high-tech lair in the Shenandoah Valley of Virginia that housed cyber supersleuths and the warriors who did the dirty bloody work in the field. Off the record, Brognola was liaison to the President of the United States who green-lighted missions for Bolan and the other warriors at the Farm.

This time was no exception.

Soon, Bolan was going to head south, armed with presidential carte blanche to find out if what the dead Marine had claimed about a classified base housing Arab fundamentalists was true.

But first, he had to unravel the mystery of a purported chemical weapons processing plant.

After six hours of watching and assessing, the soldier suspected it wasn't as virginal as Justice Department and FBI agents had found it a few days earlier. At last count, Bolan had tallied four men in black fatigues armed with HK MP-5s with fixed laser sights and commando flashlights, and military-issue Beretta M-9s for side arms.

The mystery hardforce hovered near what he believed was the main plant, dead center of the compound, as if awaiting orders. On the surface the compound was what it advertised itself to be, but Bolan knew all about classified bases where what the public saw was cosmetic. There was a spider web of pipelines fanning out from processing central, a main generator, and a shack flanked by panels with valves and gauges. Add four two-story storage tanks, a football field stretch of concrete warehouses with forklifts, and all of it painted Wolfe-Binder as innocuous.

The stage job pretty much ended there.

It was the runway, a long asphalt strip to the west, that garnered most Bolan's attention. The grounded black turboprop was a scaled-down, custom version of a C-130, the kind of bird he'd seen used by spooks who sometimes, in his grim experience, straddled both sides of the fence. Meaning they often pledged allegiance to something other than national security and patriotic duty.

Two armed shadows were at the lowered ramp, one of them on a radio, mouthing what Bolan assumed were orders. Unless he'd missed his guess, they were ready to load the cargo.

Suddenly, he saw two GMCs break from the west gate. They began a slow roll toward the cargo plane. A third matching ride remaining parked roughly midway down warehouse row. Other than hardforce activity, Bolan hadn't spotted any telltale signs—civilian vehicles for instance—that would betray the presence of a graveyard shift. If and when the shooting starting the absence of an unarmed workforce would make his task that much easier. And, with no guards posted at any of the four gates, the compound had an eerie, dying feel to it.

It seemed everyone was bailing what he suspected was a sinking ship.

Either the federal tour had put nerves on edge, or, Bolan thought, whoever the hardforce swore allegiance to had decided the job was done and it was time to pull up stakes. He decided to hold out a little longer before he made his move, his thoughts weighty with the few facts about this mission as he had them.

Dead intel ops overseas and at home aside, there was the matter of White House leaks. And Brognola had recently discovered the President—at the risk of perhaps his job and legacy—had pulled executive rank and created a group called the Special Countermeasure Task Force. Their function ostensibly being logisticians, intel wizards, super bodyguards. That was merely riddle number one, but for Bolan's money it would branch out into other darker areas.

Then—perhaps the kicker—there was the former colleague of the Farm's mission controller, Barbara Price. On the flight down in the Gulfstream to New Orleans, Bolan had received yet more disturbing news from Brognola. Two more suicides had dropped on the big Fed's radar screen. One of them, a high-ranking CIA official, was believed to be the source of leaks that had, directly or indirectly, caused the executions of operatives overseas—unless, of course the Company man was a sacrificial lamb. But it was the dead man from the NSA who had contacted Price with a mixed bag of fact and rumor—about missing weapons of mass destruction and his suspicions about the SCTF—that knotted Bolan's gut he was set to stumble into a deep serpent's hole. Too much coincidence and convenient dead bodies were stacking up, and it reeked to Bolan of conspiracy.

One suicide he could buy, but three smacked of staging, given the grim mystery surrounding murders that were connected, he was sure, to some lurking hydra. Bodies were turning up in a timely fashion when it appeared truth was one songbird away. A suicide note and an alleged sordid lifestyle had been uncovered to smear a dead CIA deputy chief's reputation, which, up to then, had been sterling.

A young Marine, decorated in the second Gulf war, with a wife and children, was assigned to Gitmo. He'd been transferred to the recently established and classified Camp Triangle. Returning home, armed with a nasty story about the torture and murder of detainees, he'd turned up in his vehicle—apparently on the way to the Justice Department—one 9 mm round through the head, gun in hand, a typed suicide note by the body.

The dead, for damn sure, Bolan thought, were talking to him. No witnesses, no clues, no rhyme or reason, other than someone wanted the truth silenced.

The fact the Man in the Oval Office wanted answers from outside the normal channels signaled to Bolan that perhaps he didn't trust his new and vaunted miniorg of intel geniuses all of a sudden. And if they had a reach all the way down into Brazil, as Price's former colleague had alluded…

However it all shook out, the Executioner had come to start the mission west of the Big Easy and easing out near Plantation Country with a bang.

He cradled the M-16/M-203 squad blaster, watching as four hardmen fell out of the GMCs. With an extended 40-round clip locked and loaded in the assault rifle, Bolan figured he'd hold back loading the M-203. He'd be able to choose from a bevy of 40 mm projectiles on his webbing—from fragmentation, buckshot, incendiary and armor-piercing high-explosive rounds—depending on numbers or if it looked like he needed to pack extra punch for a steel door or perhaps set off the cargo in a shock attack. He'd make the call on the spot.

For quiet kills the Beretta 93-R was snug in shoulder rigging, its muzzle extended with a sound suppressor. A commando dagger was sheathed on his right shin for the bloodier option of a slashed throat or a blade through the ribs, into the heart. On his right hip rode the big stainless-steel .44 Magnum Desert Eagle, butt aimed at twelve o'clock for a left-handed draw, just in case he needed to go double-fisted with both side arms in a pinch.

Whatever else he'd need—weapons, gear and sat link—was stowed on the waiting Gulfstream being sat on by two of three Farm blacksuits. The odd commando out was in the vicinity, ready to ride in with the SUV rental once the soldiers put in a call on the radio.

He was all set to go through the front door, but for what? he wondered.

Watching the north, east and west ends of the plant, Bolan felt more satisfied the longer he waited that once he breached the razor-topped chain link fence he would have clear sailing on the grounds. Six halogen lights topped around the fencing weren't much in terms of illuminating the perimeter. Warpaint over exposed skin to match combat blacksuit,

Bolan, a master of stealth and using the night and the shadows to full lethal advantage, would be as near invisible going in as he would get. Whomever the opposition was, they were either overconfident, abandoning the plant or both.

Only one way to find out, the Executioner told himself, and broke cover to go hunting.

HARPER FEARED the ghosts would haunt him wherever he ran, or tried to hide from the truth of the past, present and future. Brazil, his own island in the South Pacific, hell, perched on the top of Mount Everest, there would still be no washing the innocent blood off his hands, or erasing from memory the killings of ordinary folks who happened to be in the wrong place at the wrong time, or couldn't keep their mouths shut. Beyond his personal involvement in carrying out orders, there was the insidious knowledge that he was part of something so monstrous, so diabolical yet so insane it could rip apart an entire nation with ferocious anarchy.

Maybe it wasn't too late to get out, he considered, to take care of number one. He had no familial strings, some money from the operation already in a numbered account. He might make it in a far-off land, a new identity, start over. How badly did he really need to be part of the coming national, perhaps even global nightmare? How much blood did he need on his head? After all, he wasn't entirely without conscience. He was still wondering, even vaguely troubled by how many friends and relatives his recent victims had left behind—who might know something and talk—aware, then, that if official powers shone light on his activities he would find himself pleading his case before a military tribunal, tried for murder and treason.

It wouldn't be the first time he'd executed American civilians who wanted to squeal after they had sworn an oath and signed a blood contract to go deaf, dumb and blind on a black project. There were those two aerospace engineers in Nevada, one who had gone "missing" an hour before he was to appear on a cable documentary about UFOs and reverse engineering. And there was that microbiologist, his wife and their teenaged son in Sacramento....

Yet three more civilians here in Louisiana. Two of them had been paid a midnight call, pals of the assistant manager who had sounded the alarm to the FBI. More food for the bayou, he thought, if he wanted to be callous about it, smart if he wanted to congratulate his foresight on getting their home and cell phones tapped, bugs planted under their roofs, which had betrayed loose tongues. If the others wanted to flap their gums—the science crew included—they would turn up victims of any number of creative accidents.

Snowing the G-men from Washington wasn't that difficult, he reflected, pleased with himself for giving an award-worthy performance as the plant's manager, all the bogus credentials and manufactured background checks holding up to their intense scrutiny. After all, Wolfe-Binder had been a legitimate industrial chemical plant. The paperwork he showed them was in perfect order when they trooped in, armed with suspicions and warrants. Before their arrival it had been a little tense, he granted, a few frenzied hours of sanitizing, loading up the eighteen-wheeler with contaminated tubes, vats, the disassembled decon chamber, HAZMAT suits, weapons and so forth.

The job here was finished, at any rate, he thought as he gave a last look around.

He stepped through the front door of the main plant, leaving it unlocked. The shop was barren except for a few stainless-steel tables. The documents that could tie him to their people in Brazil and Washington had been shredded. Computers and sat links were already on board their winged ride. Nothing was left now but to roll the last fifty-five-gallon drums into the bird and set off for Brazil.

Marching past the steel facades of the giant storage tanks, he heard engines grinding to life around the corner of the first warehouse. Forklifts geared up to haul the pallets—shipped back in by tractor trailer after the Feds had cleared out—and then they'd be done.

Then what?

He shuddered at the thought of what lay ahead. Knowledge alone damn near told him he should hijack the transport bird, fly for parts unknown. His orders were to return to Washington. The big event was down to a few days, which meant his every breath would be counted by the men in the shadows. What madness did the future hold? How did they intend to actually pull it off?

He was envisioning every doomsday scenario—personal and otherwise—when he thought he glimpsed a darting shadow, east, in the latticework of pipelines. Heart racing, he feared the Feds had decided on a surprise return. Submachine gun in hand, he set off on a course between two tanks, thinking if it was an intruder he could intercept him. If it was a small army of Feds, there would be no choice but to start gunning them down—a murderous fighting evac, all hands blazing away while attempting to load the bird.

He eased into the no-man's land between the massive bins, then began rolling hard. Weapon extended, thinking he should raise his crew, gathering more speed as he reached the corner, he was crouching, going left, when the sky crashed down with a light show that exploded in his eyes. Something that felt like a sledgehammer, but what he knew was a fist, had dropped him on his back. The world threatened to black out next, as he felt himself being dragged along the ground by the shoulder.

The voice of doom helped sweep away the mist in his

sight. Looking up, he stared into the bluest eyes he'd ever seen, two chips of ice more like it, he thought, framed in combat cosmetics.

A NO-SHIT DEAL.

The armament, for one thing, told him the hitter was no G-man. Then there were those damn eyes, pinning him with judgment day, like he was a bug about to be dissected by righteous anger alone. Vaguely he was aware he had been dragged into the cubbyhole near the readout shack. Out of ear- and eyeshot of the others, no doubt. The sound suppressor threaded on the end of the big Beretta and aimed square between his eyes warned him his life hung in the balance. He glanced to the assault rifle with the attached grenade launcher in the hitter's other hand. No, the man wasn't any Fed.

"I don't like repeating myself," he heard the man's voice state. "How many, including yourself?"

"Eleven," he answered. "Thirteen, if you count the pilot and copilot."

"What's the cargo—and don't tell me it's pesticide."

Why not answer the man? Whomever he really was, Harper had seen enough black ops to know the invader had come to close down shop, more than likely with a body count as icing. In some strange way, he felt relieved, absolved of his sins, free to talk. His gut told him he wouldn't be led away in cuffs. He was no defeatist, but for some time now he'd been wondering when someone, somewhere from some No Name Agency would smell them out. In reality, there was no such thing as a secret if more than one individual knew. He was glad it was over—unless the big guy had come alone. If that was the case, he was either crazy or suicidal to tackle that many professionals, all of whom had nothing to lose and everything to gain if they stayed in the game.

Harper chuckled. "You're not going to believe me, pal, but it is, in fact, pesticide."

"You're right, I don't believe you."

"You want to go uncap one of those drums they're moving and take a deep whiff, be my guest. It's a superhybrid DDT, in gel solution. One sniff upclose and you're choking on your own vomit. If you're what I'm thinking you are, then maybe you have some idea of what that means."

"You're telling me you're cutting out a couple of steps for a nerve-gas recipe."

"Give the man a first-class round-trip ticket to Hawaii."

"Where's it headed?"

"Brazil."

Harper felt his heart lurch as something angry danced through those eyes.

"Who do you work for?"

"Uncle Sam," Harper said, and immediately regretted the answer as the muzzle dropped an inch or so closer to his face. "We're a black ops arm of the NSA."

He was poised for the next question, but the man in black was a blur, hurling himself to the side, wheeling toward the pipeline. Harper glimpsed the red beam knife through the shadows in the space the invader had vacated, heard the brief stutter of the gun. The bullets were tearing into his chest, piercing him before his mind registered what was happening. He caught his cry of pain, clinging to anger at whoever had gone for broke, missed and nailed him instead. As the life leaked out of him and the sickening wheeze of a ruptured lung swarmed his ears, he heard a howl of agony and grabbed a final look at the shadow toppling beyond the pipeline. Fading into warm blackness, aware the big hitter had chopped his friendly killer off at the ankles, he then began sinking deeper into the dark abyss, to the evanescent roar of the invader's M-16.

6

The picture always brought on the ghosts. He was not a sentimental man by any stretch, but one horror from the past had, he believed, reshaped his destiny.

And often from out of tragedy the ultimate warrior-king, he thought, was born.

He sat at the table, staring at the pretty smiling brunette with her arm around the gangly teenaged boy, wondering if the Eiffel Tower in the background was the last sight they took in together before it happened. Sipping from the glass of Dewar's, he found it strange how the bitter pain he had once felt over the untimely deaths of his wife and son from so many yesteryears had morphed him from a mere NSA operative working at the American Embassy in Paris that day to a warrior-king of the twenty-first century who was now on the verge of leading an entire nation into a new age.

With a little luck and a lot of daring, perhaps the world would be his.

As it usually happened, alone in his room, dead of night at the Embassy Suites, his private sanctuary away from the grind of White House duty, a part of him began longing for the simpler times of youth. Working for the NSA, he reflected, left virtually no room for a stable family life, especially since he'd been in charge of some of the most classified intelligence-gathering operations. They often pitted his wits and guile, not to mention his life, against everything from Colombian drug cartels to Arab terrorists to the Russian Mafia. Always on the move, watched by both the good and bad guys, sometimes it was impossible to distinguish the two sides. He was always looking over his shoulder for the silent lurking killer. Always afraid for the welfare of his family. Still, there had been many close moments shared with his wife—a loyal and devoted companion who had never complained—over the secret years. Regular vacations to some of the most beautiful beaches in the world with Tina and Rob had been stolen treasures he would never again know. Oh, the plans he had for his son's future, an academic genius, bound for the best college, the children—grandchildren—he was robbed of…

He killed the drink, topped out another from his rapidly depleting bottle. They said anger came from three sources— not getting what one wanted or thought was deserved; disappointment in or over love; and a raw burning over clear and present wrongs in the world.

Figure he was good for two out of three.

The red light on his sat link, he saw, was blinking, but he was expecting news, on several fronts. Putting the picture away in his briefcase slot, he silently cursed the traitorous snake who had leaked the agenda of his family that day. As it turned out, the Russian Mafia had put out the contract on his family, and his own head. The snake in question, he remembered, had been a colleague who had fallen prey to greed, ambition and chasing his own prurient interests, giving the Russian gangsters they had been monitoring as they made in-roads into Western Europe to expand their empire, all the blackmail leverage they needed.

One bullet to the backs of each of their heads. To this day he still hoped it was quick and painless, certain it was, but it was small damn comfort. Taking care of the snake personally had not only kept the NSA leak from the public eye, but it had put him on a new course, a changed man with nothing to lose, but who instantly came to believe in one immutable fact of life.

Human nature, at its core, was dark and selfish.

Over the years since the murders, learning what he had about the critical mass building across the planet, he believed humankind was doomed to self-destruct. Truth be told, he knew Armageddon was already in progress. The dark light of personal tragedy, he concluded, was that it had blessed him with new vision for the future of the human race—or what was left to obey and serve.

Anger, he decided, wasn't such a bad emotion, after all.

Suddenly, he felt very much alone, couldn't help but wonder if his chosen profession had, in short, caused the murders of his wife and son. Or was he destined for something greater than any human being could fathom? Was tragedy merely a small price to pay for the crown of conquest? Was he even being guided along by divine intervention? He pictured himself, standing alone in a raging sea, going down— the flaming sword of righteous anger and revenge extinguished as the churning waves enveloped him.

It was the booze, he told himself, talking back to him, depressing his warrior spirit with guilt and regret over that about which he could do nothing. Deep breath, then. Summon back the courage and resolve. It was time to move forward. His thoughts cleared.

He scrolled through the digital readout on one of four minimonitors on the sat link, waiting until all the back-channel numbers ran through before they were automatically erased from the microchip's memory, then he punched on the scrambler, settled the link around his ears, adjusted the throat mike.

"We may have problems," the voice said.

Lee Durham grunted, recognizing the voice on the other end even though it was electronically altered. He was not in the mood to hear about problems, since each member of the operation was expected to carry his own weight, and then some. In their world there could only be solutions.

"I heard," he replied.

"What's the story on your end?"

"No story, but I'm picking up certain bad vibes from the Man. He's gone out of the loop where your situation is concerned, but that much is obvious. Whoever is on the way down there I have no positive confirmation as to identity. Assume black ops. There have been rumors for years now that each administration accesses such individuals to do the kind of jobs best left out of the public eye and the Capitol Building. Deniable expendables."

"I know the breed. Are we compromised?"

Durham took his time answering, working on his drink. Firing up a smoke, inhaling deeply, he said, "If we were, we wouldn't be talking."

"Unless we're being used as the chum."

"That's crossed my mind. You are to proceed as planned, but I would suggest you learn whatever you can from the contaminants, however you can, in the next hour or so. Do whatever it takes. Are you sanitized for your visitor?"

"As well as could possibly be expected given the circumstances. There's some walking wounded that may put my butt to the official fire."

"I'm sure you'll come up with a plausible explanation—an attempted breakout, one of your men attacked, something along those lines. Concentrate hard right now and continue your work. Turn up the heat by any and all means. You—we—need a contact over there, even if it feels unreliable. Whatever the feeding chain, get something, even a guppy, until you can work your way up to the big fish."

"I know what we need."

The colonel, Durham thought, was getting testy. Certainly he could imagine the pressure he was under. Some operative not even SCTF could find a background on was flying down to Camp Triangle on a classified military flight. Snooping around, he'd be looking for evidence, no doubt, that the Geneva Convention didn't even rank a paper tiger. Now was no time, though, for excuses, waffling, wringing of hands.

"What if—"

"Stop right there," Durham said, washing the sat link with a wave of smoke. "We are too far along to cave to phantom trouble at this juncture. This was always a mobile operation. Do whatever is necessary regarding the man from Washington. Worst-case, dispose of the matter, pack up—but do not, I repeat, do not do that unless you have hard intelligence regarding the vanishing act."

"And when you've wrapped up the operation on your end, we're all expected to pull a Houdini?"

"That's one way to look at it, but you knew this going in," Durham said.

"And the money?"

Ah, and there it was.

Before anyone for Task Force Talon was recruited, Durham had anticipated some or all of them displaying a mercenary nature. Most of them had personal, professional and financial problems, all of which now drove them to flee a hell created by their own hand while skipping off for the golden sunset of a new world, armed with money, chasing whatever their pleasure to the grave. Where he was moving ahead with the event out of nobility and patriotism, skewed as some might perceive it, the bottom feeders were getting antsy for personal results. For the most part they were brutal men, useful, yes, when it came to doling out violence, creating mayhem, even getting answers under torture where other more civilized methods failed. But there was a limit to his patience, and he would not allow any man's single selfish desire to erect a barrier in front of his task.

Durham fought to keep the edge out of his voice. "Colonel, my ambitions, as grandiose and hideously incomprehensible as some in the know might find them, will play out once the package is delivered on my end. So, if anyone is actually on the firing line and potentially circling the drain, it is me and my two immediate colleagues. The package will be at my disposal any time now, so standby and await further orders once you have positive intelligence in regards to the lead in question. As for personal reward, when the time comes I will have certain accounts of our Middle East comrades, currently frozen by this administration, unfrozen and released into the numbered accounts we have agreed upon. Until then, I can only stress how important it is we let no one and nothing derail us at this critical time. Do the job, the money will be there."

He paused, annoyed at the grim chuckle on the other end. "Something amusing to you?"

"You realize the odds against you pulling it off are—"

"Yes," Durham said. He felt the flush of anger on his cheeks, wondering if the colonel was getting cold feet at this late stage. "Astronomical. However, should everyone do their part, should everyone remain resolute and committed, we will not fail. Greatness is not achieved by the faint of heart, Colonel, and revolutions generally fail when there are a few nonhackers or traitors who either go for themselves in the long run or attempt to save their own skin. Need I remind you, that if one goes down all go down. But we are not faced with some Alamo scenario."

"Yet, you mean. If this Colonel decides to phone the White House and burn the Man's ear about this base, which, by the way, he wasn't all that keen on setting up to begin with, and starts popping off about beatings and missing prisoners…"

"I am trusting you to keep that from happening. On the plus side, it is our people of Task Force Talon who are in charge down there. 'Your' people, with a smattering of Marines."

"Who could prove a pain in the ass when we pull up stake."

"Dispose of all nonessential parties, those were your orders. Remember, Washington is only sending down one man, not a platoon of Senators to comb through every piece of brush and ask a slew of questions over a few roughed up terrorists. And we have allies among the Brazilians who could assist you in the disposal area."

"Which leaves me to wonder about leaks."

Durham blew more smoke, tired of searching for the right words to calm the man with iron-clad reassurances. "The Brazilians are a greedy, thuggish lot. They only want their money. I have been in contact with Colonel Poscalar, and he's assured me, for the time being, the powers that are with us in Brasilia are quiet and cooperative."

"But that could change."

"Everything, Colonel, is about to change. See to it that whatever changes happen shortly are to our advantage. Just deal with the hand you've been dealt. Should you need an ace in the hole, the chances are good I can provide you with one. The next time we speak, rest assured the event will have started. Do your duty. That will be all."

Before Braden launched into another litany of worry-riddled questions, Durham severed the connection, shed the com link and topped out another glass. Yes, he had to agree up to a point with Braden. What was about to transpire in Washington went beyond reason and rationale, perhaps bordered on the suicidal. Still, he thought, rising, opening the door and easing out onto the hallway landing, there was no such animal as a bloodless revolution.

Changes, he decided, were coming, long overdue after forty years, thanks in no small part, to the passing of laws where wrong was right and vice versa. The country, he believed, was already clinging to the edge of the abyss, the list of ills so long it hurt his brain just to consider them.

The implosion of America was building to critical mass. There was a subtle form of evil, he thought, casting an invisible but dark pall, from Manhattan to Los Angeles. Those devils in human skin who had the money and the power to mold the masses in their image, much like any number of tyrants through the ages, were using human cannon fodder to do their dirty work. Only in America cash had replaced blood, the rich and the powerful—roughly three to four percent of the nation's population—were shearing the sheep of hard-earned dollars. The shadow of wickedness had spread over every institution, until a quicksand pit of graft and corruption, it seemed, was swallowing government, military and business leaders interested in only fattening their pockets and holding onto power.

No more.

Nothing short of a big bang change, right around the corner, he knew, would set it right, back on track, where men of reason and principle called the shots for the worker ants. Someone had to step up, save the country before it was too late. Nothing short of anarchy in the streets—followed by martial law then military rule—would stop the barbarians at the gates of a crumbling civilization. In some strange way he was almost glad he was without family. No blood lineage of his needed to fear where the future was headed, if, in fact, there was any future left to save.

Durham stepped up to the rail. Looking three floors down he watched them scurrying through the atrium, the restaurant courtyard, the lobby still bustling with late-night arrivals, kids in bathing suits running amok after a dip in the pool, couples strolling arm in arm, all of them oblivious, content. They were his sheep, he thought, about to be led to the slaughter, where Darwinian anarchy would rule before he arose from the ashes of the coming conflagration, the new phoenix, riding on wings of fire and righteous anger. He knew every revolution required sacrifice if it was to succeed so that greatness could shine.

It wouldn't be much longer now, but he knew he would barely sleep, forcing himself to perform important but mundane duties for the President and his minions until the hour of truth shook the country, perhaps seized the whole world by storm.

7

A body count was not the Executioner's primary goal, at least not going into the compound. Bolan needed answers, names, clues to a litany of nagging questions and suspicions that now appeared to reach from Washington to Brazil. He had some loose pieces of the puzzle to work with, if nothing else—high grade DDT—two or three steps shy from being morphed into nerve gas—leaving the country on a classified military flight, but what was he up against once he was southbound? And where the hell was the lethal cargo really slated to go? Into whose hands would it eventually fall?

Only time and spilled blood, he concluded, would tell.

Mystery hardman number two came close, but the Executioner's combat radar, not to mention the warning whiff of cigarette smoke, had galvanized him toward the threat on his rear. A sweep of M-16 autofire at the ankles had toppled the hardman into view beneath the pipeline with a vicious curse, and Bolan cleaned his clock with a 3-round facial that left no doubt about a closed casket viewing. Two down and, taking a dead man's word, eleven armed threats in the vicinity, the alarm of weapons fire blew the roof off stealth, and the chance of grabbing up another prisoner.

No problem, Bolan figured, he'd take them the hard way.

Bolan put an HE round down the gullet of his M-203. Checking the steel tangle of outreaching pipelines but finding no armed shadows as he rounded the storage tank, he took in the numbers around the forklift. He had come in from the east, figured to roll up the enemy's rear as he made his way west. Why not keep on banging?

Four hardmen were grouped around the GMC, with a driver on the forklift, a pallet packed with four fifty-five-gallon drums, wound together with wire, wrapped in thick plastic, right in their faces.

Perfect.

Behind him, the Executioner heard the static snarl of a voice barking over a radio. Angry words whipped away into the dark as they fell on dead ears. Ahead, men were shouting at one another, into handheld radios, HK subguns swinging toward the tank. West, Bolan found the other hard force frozen near the transport's ramp, a handman in black hollering something at his forklift driver heading across open ground.

First come, first served on the way out the gate.

The Executioner slipped his finger around the M-203's trigger, just as one of the warehouse crew spotted him in the deep shadows beside the tank. The man was waving at the others, pointing out the threat, drawing a bead with his weapon when Bolan caressed the trigger. The 40 mm comet shot forth, trailing smoke and flame. The voices downrange raised in panic as they scurried from ground zero. Impact blew a saffron fireball through the drums, and the screaming of men in agony began in hellish earnest. The poisonous contents of the drums spewed over the hardmen. The pungent stench of chemicals pierced Bolan's nose even at a sixty-yard distance.

Showered by toxic rain, hit square in the eyes or sucking down a lungful of the ghastly stew, three of the five men flailed on the ground, gagged and choked out. With shock from the blast and flesh shredded by shrapnel to sponge up more poison, they were checking out fast. They were limp by the time Bolan forged ahead.

Holding back on the M-16's trigger, Bolan tagged two hardmen still in the fight. Shooting blind, growling curses, their ravaged frames most likely being eaten up by burning poison, they swept the ground before Bolan, rounds whizzing past his ears, tattooing the wall behind him in a rolling steel drumbeat. Raking them left to right with a tempest of 5.56 mm rounds, knocking them down, Bolan fed another HE projectile into the M-203.

Hardforce Two didn't come running as Bolan veered a course well away from the outer limits of the toxin still raining to earth. They were in high gear near the transport, hardmen flailing about, arms flapping at the driver, two shadows on the ramp vanishing into the belly of the bird.

The flight crew, he reckoned, running to crank on the turboprops.

They were rattling off streams of automatic fire by the time Bolan hit a crouch beside the empty guard booth.

No prisoners, no escape.

The Executioner squeezed the launcher's trigger, aiming for an encore pesiticide detonation. As the booth began to take hits, in a whirlwind of glass and wood slivers, Bolan scored the curtain call. The blast hurled drums and searing toxic rain into the air, the forklift flying off the ramp on a gust of flames, its driver loosing a scream of agony that told the others he was going the way of sprayed bugs. A few more human insects added to the chorus of shrieking as they were doused, weapons falling silent as they became more concerned about breathing and finding a way to extinguish what was liquid fire.

Dumping an incendiary round down the launcher's chute, checking his rear but finding only the scorched dead, the Executioner rolled out through the gate. Closing on the hideous choking, two shadows flailing on the ground like gutted fish, Bolan heard the turboprops whining to life. On the march, he spared the hackers a mercy burst, then turned death sights on the transport. Judging the size of the tanker trucks near a lone hangar, and the distance to reach Brazil, he figured the wings were topped off with fuel.

Why not end it? There was tomorrow, and another battlefield, he suspected, that would demand his lethal skills. Traitors like here, too, that would demand his full vengeful attention.

Bolan cut the gap to about a hundred yards, but pushed out to the north before lining up the port wing for the final touch. He cut loose, the missile sailing on, waiting…

Bingo.

A brilliant wave of thundering white fire sheared off at least half the wing, white phosphorous igniting high-octane fuel in a blaze that appeared to take on a life of its own as it raced for gorged tanks. Bolan squinted, then turned away as the doomed ship belched apart in a fire mountain, vaporizing all life on board or maybe still clinging to the ghost on the ground.

All done here, he reckoned, as he reached for his radio, wreckage pounding the earth beyond his rolling safety zone with seismic tremors.

Quickly, the Executioner melted into the shimmering shadows, putting behind one world on fire, in search of yet another hellzone sure to come.

8

Jabir Nahab was braced for another beating. This was his second trip to the white room, but something in its appearance and in the demeanor of the American interrogator who called himself a closer had changed. Was he being set up for a new tactic? The friendly approach, all understanding and sympathy, warming him up for a sucker punch to the teeth? Did this infidel think him a fool?

He had traveled this road many times, but from the driver's side, of course. He had employed every angle, trick, deceit and psychological ruse, inflicting untold pain and mutilation on rival Arabs and traitors among his own ranks to get information, or make an example. He knew the torture drill so well, he figured he could have scripted a dozen or so new and creative sadistic and agonizing games for the infidel. But he was prepared to go to Allah at the hands of his enemies. Yet, there was something in the air, something as different as life, say, was to death. He was curious, or was he maybe hopeful?

He sat, hands and feet chained to his waist, felt sweat-tacky flesh sticking to his orange jumpsuit, watching the American working on his cigarette, a strange calm for an aura. Nahab wondered when the fist would slam his jaw or tear open an eyebrow. He glanced around the cell, revelation suddenly dawning on him why the room was different. For one thing, the plastic tarp, meant to take spilled blood and thus relieve a Marine from janitor duty—or roll up a corpse to be dumped far away—was gone. The steel chair with its head brace and eye clamps had been replaced by a simple folding chair. A small rectangular table was positioned directly in front of where the hot seat had been bolted down. The air conditioner was still in place over his right shoulder, a silent metal box he expected to start humming out bitter cold air any second. Another trick? If so, he was grateful for the moment it wasn't pumping out icy waves that, he recalled, had nearly frozen him to death when he'd been left alone with the screeching music cleaving his senses, the white light— like staring into the sun—drilling into his eyes, lancing his brain with invisible fiery needles where he sat in his own running blood from the brutal fist to his nose.

That was it! The wattage bathing him from above was no stronger than a night lamp. But when would it flare on like a supernova?

"You want a smoke, Jabir?"

Nahab hesitated, thinking this act of generosity contrived to soften him up before the fist flew. He watched the American with the bullet head, buzz cut and eyes that were all anger and shades of the ghosts of violence pop the lid on a can of soda and set it on the table. The closer held out the pack, nodding at the beverage.

"Don't worry, Jabir, it's not poison, LSD or truth serum."

With his nose smashed and blood clotting his nostrils, it was difficult to smell, but he made out the bite of bleach, maybe disinfectant, used, no doubt, to wash away the blood of whomever the previous victim had been. Something, he decided, had happened in the past few hours to dull the edge on the man's savage touch. What? And did it matter? He was still a prisoner of the infidels, far removed from his homeland of Syria. Yesterday, today, tomorrow if he was lucky, he'd still be steaming in anger and anxiety in solitary confinement through the endless hours of harassment, one cup of mealy broth and a cup of tepid water as daily ration, wondering if he'd live out the next few minutes. Or when the next round of torture would begin.

"Go on, take it. No tricks. I'm not going to lay a hand on you."

Nahad flinched as chains rattled and he stretched his hands to take the cigarette. He was steeled for a slap to the cheek, but the infidel simply lit his smoke. Keeping his tone level, he said, "Is this what you call good cop?"

"No, Jabir, this is straight man-to-man, or warrior-to-warrior, if you will. Things have changed. Listen very carefully. Your life and your freedom depend on your final answer."

He watched as the infidel stepped back, puffing hard on his smoke. Two clouds—two warriors, he thought—sharing a moment of silence, meshing their smoke, thinking, waiting. One and the same, he wondered, even if they were on opposing ends of the spectrum? Despite adversarial ideologies, and who wielded the power of terror right then, he began to wonder just how different they were in the final analysis. They warred, they killed, they wanted to live to fight another day.

They both wanted to win, if not in a mere contest of wills then facing off on the battlefield.

The closer began, "I don't like what I've done here, Jabir, all this blood and brutality on my hands. Believe it or not, there's a part of me that's almost human—let's just say I can feel your pain, your fear, your desire to breathe free air again. The deal I first put to you still stands. Give me something, a name of a contact, a general location of what you know I want, and you walk. Same for the rest. Cooperate, go with the program, I'll even fly you home personally."

Nahab chuckled, leaned forward and took a sip of cola. "Tell me why I'm not convinced by this sudden conversion."

The closer cleared his throat, began pacing, a dark look shadowing a face sharp as the edge of a razor. "There is a man coming down from Washington. Seems he's coming to take a look around Camp Triangle. He will probably question you and the others. Information on operations you may be aware of, locations of cells in America and so forth, but I'm thinking he wants to see for himself—and report back—how you and the others have been treated."

Nahab managed to keep the smile off his battered lips. "I see."

The closer, he saw, waved a hand at his face, said, "When he questions you about the facial rearrangement, you are to tell him you and a few of the others attacked your guards, a savage attack, mind you. It was in an attempt to break free and you nearly succeeded. You were clawing for eyes, balls, trying to rip out throats, hell, use your imagination, but make him a believer in the story."

"And when he inquires about the disappeared?"

"You don't know anything about that. I'll handle that problem, for all you know you believe they were released and shipped back to their country of origin."

"And in return for all this charity and forgiveness you demand of me?"

The closer bobbed his head, blowing smoke out his nostrils. "Officially Camp Triangle, Jabir, does not exist. We are planted smack up the anus of the world, even Allah would have to check a map and GPS to find where we are. We are surrounded, my Syrian friend, by corrupt policemen and Brazilian military officers who have their hands out for everything and anything—money, drugs, from kidnapping children for sex slaves to harvesting dead bodies so they can sell the organs. We have major narcotics traffickers, organized crime, Muslim fundamentalists, rebels scattered from here clear into Paraguay, police death squads and right-wing racist groups who think the only good Indian—or, in your case, an Arab—is a dead one. Everything in this area called the Triangle is for sale, and life is only as good as what a man can provide, or give up—or take for himself. That in mind, Camp Triangle was created, is being run by men who, much like yourself, are seeking the overthrow and perhaps destruction of the United States."

The closer continued. "I have been a soldier for almost two decades, Jabir. I used to believe in my country. I have fought, killed and have nearly been killed on more occasions than I can count defending America—or some ideal I used to think I believed in. Freedom and truth and justice for all and such bullshit. No more. I'm still a soldier, but I'm fighting a different war. The men I'm involved with want what's in Turkey, but that's only the beginning, only one card on the table for them. Call me a traitor, but I see myself as a warrior who wised up, jumped the twenty-first century *Titanic* that's America. I'm going for number one, that's who I'm fighting for. My soldiers and I want money, the men above me want power and dominion, but that's their business. You want to be free so you can carry on your jihad.

"I have no problem with that, I have no love for America, at least not the one I presently see. Already we have learned of several operations you or your fellow jihadists had in the works, dirty bombs to be touched off in several American cities, martyrs going down in blazes of glory for Allah while shooting up shopping malls, restaurants, resort hotels and casinos. Those plans have been scrapped, but I know there's more big events being hatched. Bottom line, Jabir, I'm here to see you go free, to have your dream come true."

The closer stopped abruptly. Stunned, Nahab didn't know what to believe. He knew, though, where there was passion, or at least the clarity of anger, there was the fire of truth. Clearly, the closer was in charge of an outlaw operation, which, if found out, could well land him in the white room, in the chair, staring into the blinding supernova, mind and spirit to be cracked like eggshell. A live or die deal was being put to him. Nahab had his answer ready.

"It's your call, Jabir. Freedom to unleash jihad again—or never see what's beyond these prison gates. How can you trust me? You can't. But you can't afford not to."

"The others?" Nahad asked.

"I've spoken to all but four. They're in. They want out of this hellhole. They tell me you can give me what I need to know, so all of us can eventually go our own ways, but only after I've finished my mission here and you or some contact of yours can deliver the goods. What's it going to be?"

Nahab took his time answering. He furrowed his brow, pretending to ponder his fate. He dumped his cigarette in the soda can, asked for and received another, the closer lighting him up. He let the infidel wait, thinking the American spoke at least some truth. Trust him? Never. Work with him, bide his time, sharpen his blade, then when he was ready to carve his own pound of flesh...

Nahab forced a smile he didn't feel. "I have two contacts, reliable. I know where they are, or how to find them. But I and the others need to be free."

"If it checks out, or if it even has a ring of potential, we're on our way to the Promised Land."

"One is in Turkey, and one is right here in this region you call the Triangle."

9

The Executioner deplaned to an empty airfield. Considering the nature of his "official" objective—an investigation into alleged torture and murder by American fighting men and intelligence agents against Muslim fundamentalist enemy combatants—he hadn't expected the red carpet treatment. But they'd been cleared for landing via a preset encrypted message to both the camp's communications center and control tower a good fifty minutes earlier. There was no welcoming committee on hand, not even a Marine or a Task Force Talon underling shipped out to greet him. The first warning signal flared up for the Executioner.

Colonel Braden Stone from Washington was a leper. And perhaps even considered the enemy.

As the Gulfstream C-20's twin Rolls-Royce turbofans shut down, Bolan walked a few steps across the runway, stopped and took in Camp Triangle. During the haul from New Orleans—roughly four thousand miles and close to eight hours—to this cleared-out stretch of subtropical rain forest hugging the borders of Argentina and Paraguay, Bolan had updated Hal Brognola, who had promptly marched in a Justice Department special task force to secure Wolfe-Binder on the heels of Bolan's evacuation. With both of them in the dark where the mission was headed, Bolan left the big Fed to the chore of nailing down seen and unforeseen logistical headaches, and to cover all the right bases, official and otherwise.

The longer he waited for some sign of life to step out into the morning sun, the more Bolan's gut warned him his visit could go unofficial in a hurry.

So be it.

One piece of the jigsaw at a time. After the slaughter and hanging questions in the wake of New Orleans, Bolan had landed in the Triangle prepared for the worst.

Nothing new.

The Farm's intel package included detailed satellite imagery of the compound, with every road, highway, trail and bridge that led to and from the borders with Argentina and Paraguay and then points north and east, thrown in for good measure, in the event an unexpected sojourn was required. The imagery, Bolan knew, was pirated from a National Reconnaissance Office satellite, but at first pan Bolan found the space shots on the money. The one-story prefab concrete building, its roofline bubbled with radar and satellite dishes, was the detention center, the rectangular structure, he recalled from grid markings, taking up close to a city block. What was inside, Bolan thought, was another matter altogether.

The Executioner snugged the dark aviator shades tight to his face. To the east, he saw a squat concrete block running about fifty yards, north to south. Intel stated the building was Camp Triangle's depot. Taking up one corner of the structure was a motor pool, filled with a half-dozen Humvees with mounted TOW antitank missile launchers and .50-caliber machine guns. There were also a matching number of black GMCs. Three forklifts parked on the opposite end, though, commanded a few seconds worth of Bolan's speculation, as the ghosts of Wolfe-Binder danced over his shoulders.

Guard towers, he noted, loomed from each of the four corners, rising ten feet above twenty feet of chain-link razor-topped fencing that enclosed the detention center and depot. With spotlights in each watch station, they likewise housed .50-caliber machine gun nests encircled with sandbags.

Surveying the vast and all-points fenced-in acreage of airfield, Bolan counted two Bell JetRanger choppers and an equal number of Black Hawks, Hueys and twin-engine Cessnas to the east. The odd bird out was a custom black-hulled spook transport, grounded with its nose aimed through the open doors of a massive hangar. Add the number of fuel tanker trucks he'd seen before landing that lined the south facing of the warehouse…

Interesting, he decided. For a classified detention center that only housed twenty-five prisoners—with more ostensibly on the way from Gitmo, Iraq, Afghanistan or wherever first-tier Islamic militants were captured by American special ops or CIA operatives in the war on terror—Bolan found it quite an impressive feat on such short notice, if Brognola's timeline for the construction of Camp Triangle was correct.

And that left the human—or inhuman—factor.

Whatever he'd perused in the official military jackets on the two main players sharing command—General Max Compton and Colonel James Braden—Bolan had decided to reserve judgment. Despite their sterling careers on record—complete with honors, medals, all the glory trimmings of heroes in uniform—Bolan's grim experience had long since dictated there were always blanks to fill in with few exceptions, when it came stamped classified or black ops.

"Colonel."

Turning, Bolan found a blacksuit squeezed in the hatchway. The C-2O was custom-built for the purposes of Stony Man missions. Inside, two-thirds of the fuselage was outfitted as a high-tech communication, surveillance and tracking center. As planned, Bolan would put it to the ranking powers the bird was off-limits, and that it would also double as his interrogation center for prisoners. The three blacksuits Bolan had selected from the Farm to aid and assist him for the mission were handpicked by Brognola. They were sworn to a lifetime oath of secrecy. They had their standing orders for the time being, and Bolan knew he could depend on the blacksuits, on the battlefield or working technical expertise.

"General Compton informed me he will meet you at the main North Gate marked A," Michaels said. "Two minutes, sir." Bolan caught the wry grin, as the blacksuit added, "He extends his apologies for not meeting you and for keeping you waiting."

Flashing the blacksuit a tight smile, Bolan nodded for Michaels to carry on. The Executioner took his time as he began ambling toward Gate A. For effect, he checked his chronometer. A look west, and he noted the solitary guard station that, apparently, marked the only way in or out by vehicle. Like the watchtowers, the booth was encased in black-tinted glass. Bolan knew—could feel—he was being observed.

All told, he considered, Camp Triangle was sprawling—and suspect.

Much like Brazil.

Not unlike the history of other nations—where the victors in violence and oppression dictated the terms and grabbed up the lion's share of the good life—Brazil's story was a violent one. Bolan knew that something like three percent of the population owned ninety percent of the wealth, while twenty percent were mired in extreme poverty, with another twenty just clawing on to desperate subexistence. With a population of 170 million, that left a whole bunch of hungry mouths. Crime? Misery? Desperation? How about, he thought, a raging hell on earth that kept the Devil dancing 24/7. How about eight million children living on the streets, roving gangs of urchins killing or being killed, stealing, selling everything from their bodies to narcotics to cadaver organs while ducking death squads that often doused them with gasoline and set them on fire, often simply because they were an eyesore. Bolan knew that corruption tainted everyone in authority from the highest-ranking military brass to border guards.

A grim realist, Bolan stopped himself. He knew wherever Animal Man plied the darkness of his heart on the weak, defenseless and vulnerable, there would always be corruption, brutality, tyranny, just to name of few of the ills that plagued Brazil to a demonic extreme few nations on earth could rival.

Along those lines of dark and angry reflection, he suspected that the remote bloody region where Argentina reached out to meet Brazil and Paraguay was selected for good reason.

The Triangle was known within international intelligence and law-enforcement circles as one of the most dangerous, treacherous, vicious outlaw cesspools on the planet. And Bolan knew it was a region—a bloody shadowland on the Brazilian border—where every viral strain of criminal, smuggler, trafficker, bandit, rebel, terrorist or rising dark star could take refuge and ply his cutthroat trade in the hopes of fattening illicit gains or hatching murderous plots. Provided, of course, they had ready cash, pure malice of heart, or contacts within the military, law enforcement or intelligence arenas they could grease, blackmail or threaten.

Not more than a dozen or so miles west from where he stood, the lesions of this inhumanity primarily congregated in a boomtown den of thieves and killers on the Brazilian-Paraguay border known as Ciudad del Este. Aware of its proximity to Camp Triangle, the Executioner had been informed by Brognola that the Countermeasure Task Force had convinced the President to set up classified shop there, in part, because Task Force Talon was interested in penetrating potential terror operations, or recruiting contract informants in Ciudad del Este. The argument—a strong one, Bolan had to admit—was the criminal haven was a potential gold mine for intelligence gathering on Hamas, Hezbollah, al Qaeda and other Mideast militants who used Paraguay much like the Nazis who fled Germany after World War II. Seeking asylum from their crimes perhaps, but in the age of terror plotting mass murder was more likely in the cards for the new breed of viper hiding in South America.

He could see how the SCTF had spun the web. If it was all a smoke screen for some larger insidious agenda, if they had baited, hoodwinked the President…

Bolan paused. They were five minutes into the waiting game, as the door opened on the windowless north facade. There were eight of them, slowly crossing a stretch of no-man's land, but Bolan recognized only Compton and Braden. Two Marines in dark green fatigues and carrying M-16s led the procession. The others donned the midnight-black fatigues—what passed, he knew from intel, as their uniform— of Task Force Talon. The rearguard, wielded submachine guns, their buzz cuts topped by black berets. Braden and the two unknowns flanking him toted only Berettas in shoulder rigging. Nobody looked eager to welcome Colonel Stone with open arms.

As Bolan walked slowly to the gate, one of the Marines punched in a series of numbers that electronically slid open the first of three mesh barriers. General Compton, working hard on a cigar, followed a Marine down the short chain-link tunnel, waiting while the next gate slid open. A TFT commando marched past him to key open the last gate.

Compton forced a smile that reminded Bolan of a used car salesman. "Colonel Stone. Welcome to Camp Triangle. My apologies again for keeping you waiting. We had some last-minute reports to prepare for you. It's been a busy morning already. I'm sure you're anxious to get settled in and get down to business."

Was that a scowl, Bolan wondered, that Braden flashed at Compton?

Bolan unzipped his windbreaker while Braden fell in beside Compton and the two TFT commandos picked up the general's right wing. The Executioner noted the emblems on the berets were screaming hawks in iron cast and full swoop, and he felt ice in the air. Compton, the only one of the quartet not hiding his eyes with sunglasses, started to hold out his hand when Bolan produced a thin sheaf of papers. Dumping them off to Compton, he got a nose full of whiskey fumes.

"My orders from Washington," Bolan said.

Compton quickly hid his annoyance with a tight smile. "Colonel, we already received those, and we're fully aware of why you're here. Rest assured, you will receive nothing but the fullest compliance in accord with Washington's orders."

The general, Bolan thought, was trying too hard to show him nothing, but he was telling him everything.

They were dirty. He had no doubt.

"That's just in case you lost the originals, or there's any misunderstanding," Bolan said.

Compton looked flustered, turned and introduced Braden, who threw Bolan a curt nod. Then Compton said, "This is Turkle and Hanover. They're part of Colonel Braden's interview team. The colonel and his team will gladly provide any assistance you might need when interviewing the prisoners."

A few choice remarks flew through Bolan's head, but why show his hand? Bolan sensed the nervous agitation on Compton, but he was taking a strong and unpleasant read off the TFT threesome. They were sizing him up and down, from the com link wound around his neck to the side arms, wondering. Their grim silence, though, spoke in rock concert decibels. Measure them, Bolan thought, top to bottom, a triple combo chip on the shoulder, attitude flashing him the invisible middle finger. These men were dangerous, and his first instinct told him they had something to hide.

"I appreciate the offer, but I'll be working alone," Bolan said, and laid out what he wanted. He watched the TFT trio stiffen. From immediate refueling of his craft, which was hands-off to all Camp Triangle personnel, to numbers on the keypads for all gates and doors, diagrammed around the compass and written out. He wanted keys to one Humvee and a GMC, both fully fueled and ready to go at a moment's notice. He wanted free and ready access to any aircraft of his choosing, all craft likewise topped out with fuel and shipshape.

He informed them he would begin his interview of the prisoners once he toured the facility, but it would be done on board his Gulfstream and his men would escort the detainees to and from their cells. He expected his men to be given the same no-questions consideration he would receive. Free access. Anywhere. Anything.

"Any problems with this?" Bolan asked.

For the first time Braden spoke. "Whatever makes you happy, Colonel Stone."

Bolan felt it pass between them. Cross a line, and they would have his ass, and Washington could kindly kiss their collective butts. They had their own agenda here, and Bolan suspected it went beyond gaining intelligence on terror operations through unconventional means.

"I want the processing paperwork," Bolan told Compton, "on all twenty-five prisoners. I want complete transcripts of each interview. I want the videotapes of each and every interview, all of it in my hands in the next ten minutes. And I hope you have more for me on the detainees than name, rank and serial number." Bolan watched as Compton glanced away, cleared his throat, gnawed on his cigar. "Is there a problem with my request, General?"

Compton looked at Braden, then said, "Colonel, why don't you gather up the processing paperwork and what we have on the record as far as interviews while I walk Colonel Stone through the facility."

"Don't forget those keys, and my diagram with all key-pad numbers."

Braden hesitated. "I might need a little more than ten minutes, if you want all that."

"You have twenty minutes," Bolan said.

"If you'll excuse me then, Colonel," Braden said. He wheeled and headed for the open outer gate, his comrades falling in.

Compton cleared his throat, turned away from Bolan, teeth still chomping his cigar. Right then, the general struck Bolan as a man bobbing in a sea teeming with sharks, as desperate as hell for someone to throw him a lifeline.

"If you'll follow me, Colonel."

10

"Fifty-thousand dollars is not exactly what I had in mind for an advance, nor does it make my heart sing with joy. I hope you intend to show me more than a mere pittance which, may I add, borders on insulting."

Braden chuckled as he threw a look over his shoulder at Colonel Miguel Poscalar. Poscalar was sitting in a chair in front of his desk, one silk-swathed leg crossed over the other, decked out in threads that would cost most Brazilians more than their annual wages. The dark sports jacket and matching shirt were woven from the finest silk, or so he bragged. A gold crucifix the size of a man's fist hung from the open shirt, unbuttoned halfway to his navel in neodisco fashion. With Italian loafers, a white broad-brimmed hat perched on a full head of coiffed black hair and the Havana cigar jutting out beneath a salt-and-pepper mustache, he struck Braden as picture perfect for a narcotrafficker, or officer on the take. Which, in fact, he was. The floating rumor was he was also the commander of the death squads that roved from Ciudad del Este to the slums of Rio de Janeiro. Behind Poscalar, Hanover and Turkle formed a human barricade at the door. Just in case Stone didn't find it necessary to knock, the Washington stooge would have to barge past them first.

Stooge? Braden thought, correcting himself. Whatever Stone was, Braden knew he was no inside-the-Beltway flunkie. The big SOB had a look, a way he carried himself Braden knew all too well from walking down more than a few dark and dangerous roads. The no-shit attitude warned Braden someone in D.C. believed the worst about Camp Triangle, and Stone had come to make it right. Which meant their days—now hours, in truth—had to be numbered.

Thinking he'd be damned before he let Stone cuff and stuff him, Braden returned to rifling through the pile of classified documents on the war table, determining what he would deliver to the SOB and what sensitive materials he would he shred before he walked out of his office. The processing papers were no problem, he knew. Standard write-ups, they contained that name, rank and serial number Stone had cracked smart-ass about, with country of origin, alleged ties to whichever miltant group, how each detainee was captured and so forth filling up most of the document. Then there were Defense and Pentagon memorandums confirming they had garnered hard intelligence while grilling the Warrior Sons of Islam detainees since their transfer from Gitmo to Camp Triangle. He made sure their successes landed on top, thinking Stone had to surely be aware that four major al Qaeda cells had been smoked out from Buffalo to Miami and at least two terrorist plots thwarted in the past month. If Stone was here, playing spook games and chumming the waters, Braden decided he could blow smoke in his face, too.

"You find this amusing, Colonel Braden?"

Braden ignored Poscalar as he clipped together all the materials relating to contacts, locations and satellite imagery of black ops best left for no one's eyes. Then he went to his desk and began hastily sketching out the detention center, filling in the requisite keypad numbers over each gate.

Poscalar scowled behind a cloud of smoke. "If our arrangement is to continue, Colonel, I must be compensated adequately. Without me, there would be no Camp Triangle, and since I stand between you and my colleagues in Brasilia, the peacemaker and arbitrator, if you will, to men who could terminate this base on a whim, I suggest you begin digging into your black funds coffers a little deeper, and soon. Beyond that, you have entrusted me to search out Arab militants who may have links to the prisoners here. That by itself is extremely risky. Am I reaching you, Colonel?"

Braden busied himself completing the whole package, knowing he had more problems than a slicked-up, designer-suited buzzard. The last shipment of supergrade pesticide, for starters, was not yet delivered, which, if there was a bright side, was good news. That kind of cargo would unleash a barrage of questions from Stone for which he had no good, or at best, rational answers.

As if reading his mind, Poscalar grabbed the bull by the horns. "Then there is the matter of the pesticide shipments, and yes, yes, I know what you claim they are. Nonetheless, it is costing me a small fortune alone to warehouse your cargo in Ciudad del Este. I have guards to pay, there is daily overhead to consider. There is transport to arrange. Now you tell me there will be no more shipments, but I am thinking I do not need the hassle."

And what about that? Braden wondered, grinding his teeth so hard he heard his jaw crack. Harper and his black ops crew had mysteriously vanished. No one was picking up the phone on the New Orleans end or returning his e-mail. Vanished. Ghosts, smoke blown away in the wind. Two scenarios burned his anxiety deeper on that score. Harper and crew either had been discovered by federal law enforcement as exporters—middlemen actually—of a highly toxic substance that was two to three steps at best from being refined into nerve gas, and arrested. Or they had jumped ship, skipping off with whatever cash they had on hand for the paradise of their choosing, leaving him to twist in the winds of doom.

Then there was Compton to worry about. Would the functioning alcoholic buffoon crack under pressure, confessing his own sins to save his blubbering hide from life in Leavenworth, playing the blame game from now until kingdom come, implicating everyone short of the Devil himself? And last but not least there was Stone, sure to demand—as soon as he took one look—to know why the hell there were six detainees who had faces like smashed tomatoes. If that happened...

The hell with it, he decided. The gig here at the Triangle was dead. There would be no return to Washington, much less ever setting foot on native U.S. soil again for him. Unless, of course, Durham and his spooks pulled off the big event. If they succeeded, it would prove one for the history books, no question, but Braden wasn't sure he wanted any part of their New America. As for his own bloody drama, the hard part may or may not be just ahead, but he had irons already thrust in the fire.

Nahab's information about a Warrior Sons contact in Ciudad del Este had panned out, only Braden was told to call the cutout back to nail down certain final arrangements regarding the prisoners and financial compensation. Not trusting anyone outside Task Force Talon to do what he wanted, what was necessary if he intended to survive, had flamed a plan to mind, whereby he could hedge his bets. It was time to clean up his own mess. But to do that, he needed Poscalar to cooperate. To get the Brazilian to cooperate he needed to cough up more cash.

"Colonel Braden, I get the impression I do not have your full attention," the Brazilian stated.

Braden bared an ugly grin at his comrades, but pointed at Poscalar. "This guy, this buzzard. He's got one hand dipping into about twenty billion U.S. from cocaine coming across from Bolivia, while the other hand is fisting up as much of that twenty billion in aid Washington sent down to his pals in Brasilia and he's squawking at me over a few thousand bucks."

Poscalar removed the cigar from his mouth. "Colonel Braden, are you trying to offend me?"

"You're goddamn right I'm trying to offend you!" Braden roared, pleased when Poscalar flinched at the sudden outburst. An inch of dangling ash fell into his lap, leaving the Brazilian cursing and slapping at his thighs.

"Wake up, Poscalar! It's crunch time, time to get off your silken ass and do more than whine about your wallet!" Whirling, he moved to his footlocker in the far corner near his own workstation. Unlocking it, Braden hauled out a nylon satchel and hurled it across the room. It sailed, nearly skimming Poscalar's head on the way to Turkle's waiting hands.

"Listen the fuck up, Colonel! I am staring down the barrel of a very big gun that was sent down from Washington in all likelihood to shut me down. If we're finished here, Colonel Poscalar, you and your vultures in Brasilia will probably never see the other half of that aid package from the U.S. You want more money, you're going to have to earn it."

Braden saw Poscalar was shaken into silence by his tirade, ready, finally, to listen to reason. He took his cell phone from his desk, chucked it to Poscalar. "Make some calls to your people in Ciudad del Este. I need backup. I'm going to war, and right under this roof. I know you have contacts in the death squads. You've got some real hard cases, and I hear a few of them are always on R and R in Ciudad del Este. I need as many of them as you can round up."

"You want my own men, you claim are members of death squads, men who have families—"

Braden dug into his top desk drawer, fished out two sets of keys and dropped them in his pocket. "Spare me the bullshit. Get them."

"To do whatever it is you intend requires ready cash, Colonel Braden."

"My men will escort you to any and all rendezvous points once you've made contact. They have enough in that bag to buy some cannon fodder and whatever you can scrounge up. And enough will be left over to pay you another fifty large on the spot, provided you come through. If you're smart, you will agree."

Poscalar settled back in his seat, nodding, puffing. "I assume you are going to fill me in on your plans."

"In due course."

"One hundred thousand by the end of the day's business," Poscalar demanded.

"Can you get me at least twenty shooters?"

Poscalar slit his gaze, bobbed his head. "Yes, it can be done, if the price is—"

"Another hundred grand, it is! Make it happen."

With that, Braden gathered up the batch of paperwork. At the door he handed off the paper-clipped bottom half to Hanover, who started marching toward the shredder as soon as he stepped out into the hall. Braden stole a few moments of blessed silence, sucking in deep breaths, slowly exhaling. When he felt the storm was sufficiently calmed, he began swiftly marching away from the administrative quadrant, down the corridor marked *D*. Assuming Compton began the tour from the northwest end, where the lines of holding cells began in the warehouse-style pen, he still had a couple of minutes to pull it together, get ready to fake it for Stone. He was past the open but empty shower area when he made out Compton's voice, just around the corner of the main corridor *A*.

"I have to reiterate, Colonel Stone, the breakout was an aberration. There were eight of them and only four Marines at the time. I know, Colonel, before you say it, we are only thirty-strong here between Marines and Task Force Talon, and the manual states there should be two guards for every prisoner, but that's not my call to make. Washington dictates numbers and procedure."

Braden gritted his teeth, imagining how much Compton had already kissed up to the SOB, trying so hard to snow the guy Stone had to have seen through it all like a pane of glass. He pulled up at the corner to eavesdrop a few moments, get a read on how Stone might be reacting. He heard keys rattling, cell gates opening, Stone grunting.

"Remarkably, no one was killed, but the Marines who were attacked were shipped back to the States."

Stupid damn fool, Braden silently screamed. And the man was a general? Didn't he know that was easy enough for Stone to verify with one call? What the—

"And like I said, Colonel, the reason there are only twenty-two prisoners at present is because three were released and returned to their countries of origin once Colonel Braden and his men determined they were noncombatants."

As in the ones I executed, Braden thought. He barely caught Stone sounding another grunt as the blood pressure thundered in his ears. When all else appeared on the verge of failing or was suspect, he thought, blame the other poor bastard, and in his case he was guilty as charged. Braden began to think it would be best to leave Compton behind in the ashes.

Before it got any worse—and he knew it could be a death sentence if Compton kept running his mouth—Braden rolled around the corner. He saw a lean shooter in blacksuit with a briefcase in one white latex-covered hand vanish into one of two open cells. He wondered who he was and what he was doing. He saw Compton throw him a worried look as he closed the gap and an orange jumpsuit in chains duck-walked into view. Stone was taking his first prisoner for grilling.

And, of course, Braden saw, it had to be Jabir Nahab.

11

Plan B was never far from the Executioner's thoughts, and it went way beyond the official boundaries of any military protocol.

It didn't take a world-class investigator to see Braden and his bullies had used seven of the twenty-three detainees as punching bags, clearly violating the Geneva Convention where the rules of handling enemy combatants was concerned. Worse, he strongly suspected Braden or one of his interrogators had executed the three missing prisoners—whether as examples to the others or something else—and Compton's flimsy explanation fairly sealed Bolan's hunch.

Torture and beating of enemy combatants was not part of the warrior's prescribed regimen, though he wasn't above inflicting pain on rare occasions to get answers when lives hung in the immediate equation and he found himself staring into the face of the responsible evil. Braden and his thugs apparently used torture on a regular, if not daily basis, as easy as breathing, and he could only imagine what the detainees had suffered at their hands. As for facing a court martial and lengthy prison sentences, Bolan suspected Camp Triangle's hierarchy had their own backup plan to escape justice, ironed out before they even landed in Brazil. So why, then, Bolan wondered, risk so much, under the watchful eyes of Marines who would go to their graves defending a uniformed code of military honor, and when they knew report of their brutal actions would eventually leak back to Washington?

The question alone answered itself, Bolan concluded. Braden or his superiors wanted something badly enough to jeopardize careers, risk prison and their own lives, and they believed one or some of the detainees at Triangle had the answers they needed. Bolan believed he was on track to solving the mystery. All he had to do, he figured, was follow—or ride—the dark horse to the finish line.

For the moment, Bolan decided to stick to Plan A. Play it hard, tight-lipped and official. Follow through with interviews. Fax all fingerprints, both Triangle's originals and those just now redone by Michaels. With those, he would also send all processing photos and documents to both Brognola and the Farm. He needed those he trusted implicitly to send back reliable intel on whatever Braden might have conveniently left out. Meanwhile he would keep Triangle's suspects dangling over the fire. If Braden and bad company sweated enough, they might crack and force Plan B into action.

Unless he missed his hunch, the Executioner believed Plan B was as close as the next few hours, or the next set of prisoners.

Bolan glanced at the two militants, both of whom had had their faces shoved through Braden's meat grinder. They were looking at him, uncertain, but Bolan thought he glimpsed something else in their battered faces. Strange, but they seemed resigned, or hopeful, he thought, unlike the burning hate, rage and defiance he'd seen countless times in the eyes of fanatics, on or off the battlefield. It occurred to him that Braden had paid all the detainees a last personal visit before his arrival, spelling out their futures if they made the evident abuse out to be anything other than a counterattack for escape. But Bolan's gut told him something else was spinning in their hearts and minds besides lies and cover stories.

While they sat, ramrod stiff, in bolted-down leather wing-
backs across from the Executioner in the Gulfstream's aft,
Bolan perused the documents on two detainees Braden had
handed off, assessing the situation, gathering more of his own
thoughts. The short time he'd spent with the hierarchy and
sightseeing the facility had only served to further cement his
grim suspicions. For one thing, Compton was so nervous he
babbled nonstop, repeating himself, every word out of his
mouth scripted for Colonel Stone's benefit, no doubt,
whereas Braden was walking body armor, not the first hint
of even a conversion of convenience. Then there was the interrogation room itself, the smell of bleach still lingering in
the air where blood had, in all likelihood, been mopped up.
There were subtle changes in the room, he suspected, such
as cracks in the concrete floor where a chair had been bolted
down. There was the air conditioner, which had been turned
off, but someone had neglected to reset the dial from HI-
COLD, if the intent had been to further try to fool him the
room had not been recently used as a meat locker. There was
the light, which would stare directly into the eyes of a detainee, easy enough to simply change the bulb, from high and
blinding, to low wattage before his coming. There should
have been video or at least audiotapes, recording all ses-
sions…

Bottom line, he decided, Braden and company were crim-
inally guilty. If it was all headed where Bolan suspected it was,
they'd be lucky to stand in one piece before a military tribunal.

After reading what little background Braden's documents
provided, Bolan looked at Jabir Nahab and Atta Dbouri. Beyond the detainees, Bolan saw his blacksuits, com links on,
hunched at the workstation. Michaels fed the fax, in communication with Stony Man Farm, while the other two relay
feeds. Tied into the Farm's own cyber link to whatever mil-

itary or spy satellite they managed to steer and park over the Triangle, the blacksuits were ready to intercept any form of communication, coming into or leaving the compound.

Bolan looked at his prisoners. "When did your attempt to break out happen?"

They thought about something, hesitated, then answered at the same time, "Two days." "Four days."

Bolan kept his expression deadpan and fired off the next question without missing a beat. "Where did it happen?"

"In the shower—" "Just outside our cells—"

Bolan flipped the mostly useless file of Braden crap on the seat next to him. "Why are you lying to me?"

Nahab seemed the most tense of the two. "Why would we lie about being beaten like this? Do you think we did this to our own faces?"

"No. I think either Braden didn't do such a hot job concocting your story, his cover story for me, or you're too nervous or scared about something to think straight and tell me the truth." Pausing, Bolan let them feel the full measure of his penetrating stare. "What is it Braden and Compton want so bad they're beating men to a pulp and even murdering your comrades?"

Whatever the truth, Bolan watched it harden both their faces.

"What did he promise you to lie to me? Freedom? Money? Weapons? All of the above?"

The prisoners were silent.

"If you have something to say, now is the time."

They glanced at each other, and for a second Bolan thought they would crack.

"He wants what all you American Special Forces and operatives want," Dbouri said. "Information regarding our ongoing operations to crush the Great Satan."

And Bolan saw defiance return to their eyes. He gave

them a few moments to reconsider, then realized they
wouldn't break. Good enough, he decided. He already had
what he wanted from them anyway. He had caught them in
a lie. In his experience, one lie always led to another, and few
human beings, save for perhaps the pathological liar or pure
sociopath, could keep all their lies straight. Eventually the avalanche of lies and half-truths tumbled toward the truth. All
Bolan had to do was keep pressing.

When the Executioner motioned for them to stand up they
looked at each other, confused and worried. "Let's get you
back to your cells. I need those seats," he said.

BRADEN CHECKED HIS WATCH. "You gotta be shitting me!
That's still another six hours, and just for a face-to-face!"

Fuming, he watched Poscalar shrug, as if to say what's the
rush, the Brazilian pouring himself a drink at the wet bar. "I
cannot control their daily routines, Colonel Braden. These
men, their world does not revolve around you. They have
their own affairs to attend to."

"Oh, I'm sure they do. Selling dope, pimping, stealing."

Poscalar removed another cigar from his gold-plated hu-
midor and placed it between grinning lips. "I was unaware,
Colonel Braden, you were in such a state of grace, whereby
you can cast the first stone."

Braden spun on the man from the far side of his desk,
seething as he watched Poscalar sip his drink and smoke.

"Two thousand per man, and not knowing what it is you
wish from them, well, you must understand they are perhaps
a bit on the anxious and cautious side," the Brazilian said with
a shrug.

Braden felt himself about to explode, thinking the list of
problems reaching critical mass had swelled to the breaking
point and he might just take it upon himself to pick up an assault rifle, march right out to their military VIP aircraft and

handle the Stone problem his way, his time frame. He was about to tell Poscalar he'd raise the individual payments another grand when his cell phone trilled. He didn't recognize the caller, but the numbers indicated the call originated from Ciudad del Este. Punching on, he recognized Nahab's contact and listened to the instructions. For once, there was news, if not good, at least positive there would be action. Confirming the instructions, Braden signed off. "Put the drink down and follow me," he told Poscalar, "you're on a revised schedule as of now."

SIX BRIEF INTERVIEWS later, Bolan knew he'd either have to change his tactical approach to questioning, or accept that Braden had influenced the prisoners to stick to the same story as the first pair, rattle off the standard jihad rhetoric or plain stonewall. In short, Bolan was getting nowhere closer to the truth.

The good news was that the blacksuits had intercepted cell phone relays to and from Braden, to and from the Brazilian military attaché who was on-site but unseen at Triangle. Bolan had never met Colonel Miguel Poscalar, but Brognola's file on the man was thick with pretty much the usual sins for a corrupt officer. Beyond drug trafficking, arms smuggling, suspicion of murder, extortion and graft, Poscalar was reputed to be Brazil's commander in chief of the police death squads. That alone, Bolan knew, should have earned Poscalar a one-way ticket to hell. But given what his blacksuits had overheard, Bolan intended to use the man as chum in the coming hours, to net and harpoon the bigger maneaters. It seemed Colonel Braden was in the process of initiating his own Plan B.

The areas in question were already triangulated down to a few square yards, in Bolan's hands, thanks to the Farm's expert handling of the spy eyes over the Triangle, and relayed to his blacksuits. Anticipating Braden to make his big move, Bolan had already given the blacksuits their next round of orders. Unless a meteor obliterated the camp and crushed the grimmest of murderous plans, Braden was poised to ship out his two brigands and Poscalar to reach out and hire cutthroats for some wet work. When that happened Bolan was prepared to go at a moment's notice.

"Are you with these…savages here?" a shaky voice asked.

Bolan dumped the space shots on the seat beside him and looked at detainee number nine. Bringing them in alone, he decided, might loosen their tongues, where they felt free to talk, and not be shackled by fear of retaliation from Braden or their own militant comrades. The Syrian's name was Mohammed Bal-Ada, and there was nothing incriminating, as far as being a terror operative went, in his file. Nor was there a scratch on his bearded face, which left Bolan wondering just how important he really was if Braden had opted for the kinder, gentler approach to this prisoner.

"No. I'm with me," Bolan stated.

The Syrian took a few moments to choose his next words. "If I talk to you…is there a chance I may go free?"

"That depends."

"Meaning is there American blood on my hands?"

"Anyone who may have died, whether you pulled the trigger, or built a bomb or helped plan an operation. Even if you were in a training camp that would cancel out any deal."

"You have ways of checking. There is no blood on my hands. And I was never in any camp. I have family back in Syria. I was a potter. My village is just north of Damascus."

"We have your file, but whatever information you can provide that helps us verify who you are, where you've been and what you've done—"

"I understand. You will check, you will find I am not like the rest."

Looking deep into his eyes, Bolan tended to believe him. "What do you have to tell me?"

"I have overheard them call us the chum, or the contaminants. It is what we are to them—bait, or some rabid animal they feel they can beat whenever they please."

"Braden?"

"Him and his two sadists. You saw the others, how badly they were beaten. Dumped like garbage in their cells. No doctor."

"Why didn't they do the same to you?"

"I do not know. Perhaps because they believed I had nothing of value to tell. Or I found the courage, through Allah, to defy them." The Syrian's gaze narrowed with anger. "They would leave us alone for two, sometimes three days, strapped in a chair, but after so long in the white room you cannot keep track of time. One minute feels like an hour, an hour like a day. Our eyelids were forced open by clamps. We just sat there, naked, this light like the sun in our eyes. American rock and roll so loud it split your brain…soon you can't stop your body from shaking…the freezing air…then you hear your own voice in your head screaming or perhaps you are screaming out loud for the noise to stop, for the light to be turned off, for the cold to end. You want to vomit, but there is no food or water in your stomach. You gag, start to choke on your own tongue. They watch for this to happen, then turn down the light, stop the noise. For a while at least." He paused, shame and rage burning in his eyes. "I thought I would go mad for days after…still thought I was in that chair. I thought I was blind when they returned me to my cell. I prayed to Allah. Slowly, my sight came back."

Bolan clenched his jaw. Whatever it took to defeat an armed enemy on the battlefield was one matter. When torturing defenseless prisoners, even ones known for committing atrocities, whether for information, out of spite, hatred or revenge… It robbed a man of his soul, reducing him to less than an animal.

Bolan had enough right there to cuff the Task Force Talon commander, shut Triangle down and bring in the Justice Department task force Brognola had standing by in Washington. He believed Braden was only a bit player in some larger and bloodier conspiracy. Leverage, then, to use on the weak link that was Compton? Bolan suspected he wouldn't get the chance.

"Go on," Bolan prompted.

"Three I know of have disappeared. They go to the white room, we never see them again. I assume they were murdered. I can give you their names."

"I already know who they are. You said they call you the chum? That tells me Braden and his people are after something either you or the others know about. What is it?"

"I was offered money by Syrian intelligence officers, but I cannot say precisely who they were. They wanted me to haul some cargo across the border into Turkey, the northeast frontier that leads into Kurd country. I am a poor man. I needed the money for my family. I did this for them, three times. When I arrived where I was told to go, there were Turk soldiers and what I learned were Iraqi fedayeen to receive the cargo. On the last trip, one of the crates, it slipped out of the hands of one of the Iraqis and broke open at their feet. Suddenly they were running away. It would have been laughable, but then I look down, I saw artillery shells, perhaps the seals have cracked. I then know what it was I had been paid to deliver."

And there it was, Bolan thought.

Weapons of mass destruction.

The revelation simply hurled another batch of questions and mystery into the picture.

It was the Pandora's box of the new century.

"You were picked up at the border coming back," Bolan said.

"By American Special Forces. I was, how you might say, in the wrong place at the wrong time."

"And you told none of this to Braden or anybody else?"

"No."

"Not even under duress, when you thought you were broken by them? Or even when you were back in your cell, maybe not clear on what was real and what wasn't?"

Bal-Ada shook his head, adamant. "No."

One of the blacksuits interrupted. "Colonel, we have a party of three, moving with purpose looks like in the northeast sector."

Bolan went to a window on the cabin's portside, aware their sensors were aimed at the motor pool. Looking out, he was just in time to spot Turkle and Hanover, each TFT commando opening the door to a GMC and piling in behind the wheel. Number Three's face Bolan had committed to memory from his intel package. No sooner was Colonel Poscalar claiming the shotgun seat in Turkle's vehicle than the GMC was lurching ahead, a Marine stationed at the northeast edge keying open the gate.

Bolan gathered up the smaller of his two war bags.

Plan B, he knew, had just gone into effect.

12

The road they took to Ciudad del Este was Brazil 277. Most certainly, he thought, their way was not paved with good intentions, if he judged the America's dark overtures accurately. For damn sure, Colonel Miguel Poscalar was in no mood for a leisurely sightseeing jaunt, if such a thing was even possible. Traffic, by itself, was hassle and headache enough. Every contraption on wheels, from donkey carts, horse-drawn taxis, bicycles to gaudy rust-bucket tour buses, clogged the main inbound artery, with enough squall, between braying animals and blaring horns, to ignite the throbbing fire behind his mirrored eyes. If that wasn't enough to keep the aggravation steaming, the driver-bagman, Turkle, wasn't inclined to answer questions, as in precisely where was their first stop and to meet whom. When he wasn't watching the GPS console mounted on the dashboard, Braden's henchman muttered curses at the congestion, or flung a monosyllabic grunt whenever Poscalar framed a question.

Bitter annoyance at being treated like a second-class citizen in his own country was serving only to swell the pulsing heat in his brain. Normally, Poscalar would look forward to a soujourn to Ciudad del Este. His familiar stomping grounds had many contacts and connections, underground and above, spread through what was known as the shopping mecca of South America. His seedy affiliations, he knew, were his primary usefulness to serve Braden. Here, they—meaning usually thieves and con artists, he thought—sold everything from watches to spiderweb lace to fake Inca artifacts, to every contraband imaginable, any vice desirable for ready cash. They also plotted, launched and commanded country, contintent and even worldwide criminal enterprises. All things considered, Ciudad del Este was the devil's playground, and woe to those who could not match violence for violence, treachery for treachery, illicit dollar for dollar. Poscalar conceded there was, however, much money to be made here, nothing but good times on tap.

Not so this night, he feared. No dice or poker, no whoring, no drinking the night away, or indulging in some Bolivian marching dust, lolling in Jacuzzi, a teenaged girl on each arm. At that moment, he found life could not seem more unjust. And Poscalar could be sure the henchman did not believe in mixing business with pleasure.

He torched a Cuban cigar with a lighter and looked into the sideview mirror. Why had the other henchman, he wondered, chosen to ride alone? Where was the commando-thug he knew as Hanover? It would be impossible to make out the duplicate GMC, just the same, what with all the tour buses, bumper-to-bumper congestion and peasants on foot, many of them human pinballs darting in and out of traffic like some game of chicken on foot. Idiot peasants. With the waning sun casting shadows over the highway, blanketing the neo-colonial dwellings dotting the hills to the north, everything began to look the same to Poscalar.

Dark and forbidding.

The henchman cursed, checking his watch. Time was irrelevant at that point, Poscalar decided. By the time they finally got their act together at Camp Triangle—callbacks and such to nail down the particulars of several meets—easing into the eastern outer limits of the city, nightfall was assured.

Whoever was waiting for the henchman on the other end would either keep, bolt, or have a few choice words whenever they arrived.

Not his problem. Or was it?

Poscalar willed himself to relax. There was the future to consider, after all, when this sordid, mysterious business with the Yankee commandos was finished. Granted, if not for his hefty cut of the U.S. aid package delivered to his comrades for their support of Camp Triangle, it would prove a monumental stretch to complete the estate he was having built outside the capital. Only four days earlier, he recalled, he was drinking tequila, a snoot full of Bolivian flake, with the architects poring over blueprints, debating how to squeeze in the horse-racing track next to the golf course he had dreamed of for years. There were other ventures on the board, to be sure, beyond erecting his own palace and personal playground, but he needed quick, fat cash to keep the dreams alive. One hundred thousand for one night's work—and this was no milk run, he suspected—wasn't going to land him the keys to his kingdom. Still, there were other financial avenues open to a man with his ambition and status, who had all the right contacts, wielded the power to back up whatever move he chose to make.

It was true, he had to admit, grimacing in anger as Braden's harsh rebuke echoed through his mind, he had made a small fortune, thanks to the Bolivian cocaine he allowed the traffickers to import across the border and funnel through his own network of distributors. If not him, he reasoned, then another officer from back east or in the Triangle region would step up and provide safe haven, free rein for the narcotraffickers to unload metric tonnage worth billions U.S. If not him, clipping about five million U.S. annually from the Bolivians—a mere pittance if he stewed about it—then his dream of owning his own hotel-casino in Rio would never see glorious fruition. If a man didn't have dreams, he thought, he might as well be dead.

Yet there were headaches and human error wherever he turned these days. Just to name one problem, there was the toxic cargo he was warehousing for Braden. The Yankee swore it was worth more than its weight in gold or all the cocaine in the Andes. That, if he could find buyers—terrorists— he could cut himself in on the sale, with Braden presumably having his own designs for a large portion of the toxic store. Swimming in shark-infested waters would be preferable in his mind than dealing with Mideast fanatics. If he was found even indirectly responsible for turning Brazil or Paraguay into Baghdad or the Gaza Strip, no amount of bribery would save him from a firing squad. Where there too many unseemly business endeavors tripping over too many unstable feet, he knew, trouble was never far behind. Was there, then, an ill wind at his own back?

One way or another, it would be a relief to hang up this night's business in the closet, get on with building his empire, securing retirement, look forward to simply enjoying the golden years of song, dance, wine, and wealth. He didn't trust Braden and his thugs any farther than he could spit. Whatever their agenda—and it involved treason of some type against their own country, he suspected—he wanted nothing more than to wash his hands of them. They were bad men, he decided, worse even than those death squad policemen he commanded, but what he—they—did was business, something of an act of salvation to assure Brazil didn't spiral into criminal anarchy, sure to be followed by a mass uprising, where revolution might find him losing more than career, wealth and status. The anxious truth was that he needed, for the moment, at least, both his death squad contacts and the Yankees.

But for how long? And to what end?

Poscalar decided his first order of business was to arm himself. What worried him the most was being kept in the dark about why and for what they needed his men. It had the foul odor of blood spilled before the night was out, and getting his own hands dirty at this stage—where the world, or his corner of it, was almost his to own—only held the sour prospect of dimming the light on his future.

Ahead, he found they were easing onto the east edge of Avenue Monsenor Rodriguez, shabby neo-colonial buildings rising down the long, wide boulevard that was choked with traffic, boutiques, sidewalk merchants and their stalls. He realized he was fingering his crucifix when he heard the henchman say, "Yes. Yes. I understand. I copy."

Poscalar saw the bagman punching the keyboard on the GPS console. It flickered into two screens, side by side, one of which Poscalar recognized as a radar monitor. Suddenly the henchman slammed on the brakes. At the last instant, Poscalar spotted a man running in front of the vehicle. He thrust a hand on the dashboard to keep from smashing the cigar into teeth, which might likewise have been snapped off. Glaring, he thought the henchman grinned, but the expression whipped away, from the rear to side view glass. When he began searching the skies through the windshield, Poscalar felt his anxiety ratchet up. Turkle was muttering into his headset how he copied, grunting, he assumed, to Braden. Poscalar checked the darkening heavens above, west and north. He thought he glimpsed a dark splotch beyond the high-rise apartments, too far north to make out with any firm detail, there then gone, but he was sure it was a helicopter.

Poscalar watched as Turkle hung the radio on his belt, one leg pressing the money bag against his seat. "Is there something you wish to tell me?" Poscular asked.

"Everything's under control, Colonel."

"Then why do you keep watching the sky? Are we being followed?"

"If that's true, it's nothing Hanover or I can't handle."

Poscalar grunted. He fingered his crucifix, suddenly wishing to a God he hadn't prayed to since he was a boy that he shared the henchman's confidence.

BOLAN WASN'T SURE WHY, but he turned south, allowing Turkle and Poscalar to go their own way for the time being. At least three stops he knew of were on the hit parade, but the Executioner had a gut feeling two or three more safehouses were going to leave bodies chalk-lined by the authorities before he evacced by chopper. Unless it went to hell on round one, and his War Everlasting screeched to its final bloody stop.

He was driving toward the deep southeastern corner of the city. He already knew who but, more importantly, what waited at the end of the line, a faint but mounting angry stir in his heart assuring him he couldn't jumpstart the blitz any more pure and right. If the promised payments matched shooters inside, Bolan figured twelve or thirteen hardmen, tops were on-site. He had a few moments to spare assessing his situation.

Michaels was left to patrol the skies and track Turkle and Hanover as best he could, but Bolan had to believe there weren't too many GMCs with blacked out windows roving the city. With his own GPS monitor, the locations of the meets already nailed down and Michaels above, Bolan knew the only factor that would keep him from a date with dispatching death was the snail's pace traffic. Or the police.

Stop number one would surely get the cannibal avalanche tumbling, he knew, but then what? It didn't escape the warrior that Braden surely knew he'd bolted Camp Triangle, now in pursuit, with questionable motives. That his quarry would be alerted they were being tracked was something Bolan counted on. Whether or not he, in fact, was being led into ambush, Bolan hoped they pushed panic buttons, just the same, started shooting without warning, erasing all gray from the equation.

Bolan took in the compound on the slow roll, unimpressed with what he viewed at first look. Nothing by way of surveillance—sat dishes or antennas on the roofline—nor even mounted cameras that he could detect on the retaining wall. It told him the targets were arrogant, had the local authorities well-greased or both. Turning into a cul-de-sac, he spotted the narrow mouth of an alley, midway around the dead end block ringed three-quarters by squat dark structures, which at first hard look appeared abandoned.

The Executioner backed the GMC into the dark void, hoping for a quick and easy getaway when the smoke began to clear. Shutting down all systems, satisfied the immediate area was free of stragglers or watching eyes, Bolan fell out. Quickly he pulled on the knee-length black leather trench coat. It was custom made courtesy of the Farm, outfitted with deep pockets and slits on both sides to store extra clips, webbing lined down each wing to hold grenades. For urban combat, passing at first glance as a regular citizen out for an evening stroll, it was as good as it would get. Weighed down and bulked out with enough ammo to start a small war, Bolan factored in a slight reduction in speed and agility. He intended to compensate for that with one last piece of hardware.

Pocketing the keys, hauling out the M-16 with full clip and a 40 mm HE round set to fly, Bolan gave the Paraguay haven for Brazilian policia militar a last look. The good news was that it set alone from other nearby structures, park and promenade, all revelry and traffic nightmares safe from collateral damage for what he had in mind. It looked to be little more than a two-story warehouse, wooden shutters closed, but two sentries were standing guard at the front door, smoking, goldbricking, passing a small tray or glass pane between them, each one taking turns stuffing a tube up their nose. The party boys, though, were armed with HK G-3 assault rifles. From the cell intercepts, Bolan had a strong clue what was inside the walls, but all questions would be answered in short order.

The Farm had managed to run down a name from the intercept with Poscalar and faxed him the cannibal's pedigree, with mug shot, spelling out his crimes and known associates likewise believed to be on the lam and inside those walls. Aside from drug trafficking, bribery and corruption, the Poscalar stooge was wanted back in Rio for multiple counts of murder. From rival drug dealers to street urchins it apparently made little difference who they butchered, and it seemed the cannibal in question had a love for setting places and things, but especially orphaned urchins, on fire.

Under the roof in this dark secluded corner of Ciudad del Este Bolan strongly suspected at least a full squad of Brazilian death squad military police was gathered. That in mind, he reached inside the GMC, delved into his war bag on the passenger floor. Why not? he decided. If he was going to make noise enough to blast open the gates of hell, why not bring his little friend to the party, make sure what went down stayed down.

Built from scratch by John "Cowboy" Kissinger, Bolan hauled out what the Farm's armorer tagged the Blaster 61. Roughly the length and look of a military shotgun, the ominous difference was the five stainless-steel cylindrical chambers attached beneath the fat bore, dead even with the trigger of the pistol grip. A crank handle near the muzzle to rotate the chambers, and Bolan could pump out the full load of 61 mm rounds in whatever desired decimating effect in about six seconds. He had each chamber slotted with HE rounds.

The Executioner hung the Blaster 61 around his shoulder.

He was marching through the opening in the retaining wall, rolling hard up the walk, M-16 hung by his leg, when the death squad duo spotted him and made their move. They were flinging away the party favors, losing the smokes and bringing their G-3s online, a noise like shock croaking from one of their mouths, when Bolan tagged them with a full-auto burst, stitching them, left to right, gouging out ragged divots in their chests. No sooner were they flopping to the ground, sprawled out on the stoop like a heap of limp noodles than Bolan bullrushed the door. A 3-round burst to the handle on the fly, shearing off metal and gouging wood where catch met jamb, and the warrior hit the barrier with a thundering kick. Two steps in, combat senses torqued to overdrive, and Bolan took in the scene.

The short hallway fanned out into a large warehouse, no doors leading the way to hide combatants, but with catwalks and offices uptop, west side. Dead ahead, at roughly forty yards, he found a group of five men, leaping from a table littered with bottles, poker chips and small mirrors humped with the white controlled substance of choice. Cards flew from their hands as they grabbed G-3s and Uzi submachine guns. And directly to their rear Bolan spotted pallets stacked with fifty-five-gallon drums.

The Executioner hung the M-16 around his shoulder, filled his hand with the Blaster 61, caressed the trigger and sent the first missile streaking downrange with a loud chug. They were hitting triggers, winging short wild bursts his way in panic-stricken hope and pray, when he scored a direct hit on the drums behind the five hardmen. The blast rocked the warehouse with ear-splitting thunder, smoke and flames shooting over the hardforce, at least three of them, he glimpsed, sailing for the roof, all screams and windmilling but mangled limbs.

Then the anticipated gruesome wrath descended.

As the toxic brew showered armed shadows the warrior spotted charging from a nearby pocket, banshee shrieks flaying the air, Bolan jacked the handle, rotated another 61 mm projectile into place and pumped out another hellbomb. No point in pulling punches, Bolan decided, no sense fretting about noise and police swarming the block.

The Executioner was moving in to run and gun, as another batch of drums puked away toxic loads on a roaring ball of fire to douse a few more cannibals in what amounted to the fires of hell on earth.

There went the neighborhood.

13

Naim Ali Zhabat, a.k.a. Andrew Zabatarsky of Poland, as stated in his passport and visa, found the infidel's offer most intriguing.

The Iraqi had the divan to himself. His men, armed with HK 33 assault rifles, grouped in twos and threes around the large living room, glaring daggers into the lean infidel with the buzzard's face framed under the black beret with swooping hawk insignia. Zhabat knew virtually nothing about the black beret, other than he helped run a classified prison across the Brazilian border. If reports from his own sources and handlers overseas and in Paraguay were correct, it was a torture chamber for fellow jihad fighters captured by American commandos. The way he heard it, they were taken by force from Afghanistan to Iraq to Turkey. From his own experience fighting the occupation forces, he had no reason to doubt the intelligence. He already despised the black beret.

The Brazilian colonel, on the other hand, was a man whose reputation for moving contraband preceded him, he knew, and Poscalar could have uses, regarding weapons, military or intelligence contacts in the city. In due course, deciding to hear the infidel out, Zhabat would determine both their fates. One might live.

Smoking, one leg crossed over the other, an arm laid atop the divan, he wanted to give the infidel calling himself Turkle the impression he was in complete control of man and moment, that maybe he needed convincing, perhaps some groveling from the American, if he was to undertake the task being proposed. He had not offered them a seat, disarming Turkle as soon as he entered the apartment, secretly enjoyed the unease. The infidel's fixed scowl told him he didn't appreciate the lack of hospitality, or found it beneath him to breathe the same air, whereas the Brazilian Colonel seemed agitated, casting glances at his fighters, as if he couldn't wait to bolt out the door.

Zhabat heard how the infidel would pay them three thousand per warrior to attack the prison, but they were to slay only the Marines, hands-off all black berets. The breach into the compound would be taken care of for them, with sabotage of the comm center assuring no SOS brought in the cavalry, but they would go only on Turkle's orders. They would see an aircraft when they hit the grounds, a VIP executive-style jet, parked near the fuel tankers by the hangar. It was imperative they hit the craft before storming the prison complex—they would get help from other black berets—and make certain all occupants, in particular a tall dark man, were killed.

Zhabat then heard Turkle rattle off a few names of freedom fighters he recognized from his own intelligence sources. It was an impressive list, he decided, of fighters sorely needed in the struggle against the infidel occupation force back home. At least two names he recognized from Mosul, where he had been previously engaged in striking back at the Americans with his small guerrilla force.

Bitter about the recent past, he recalled how his name had found its way into the hands of American Special Forces in the area, where he was branded a resistance leader, bomb maker, a savage killer responsible for many deaths of Americans and several Western journalists. An informant—shot by his own hand hours after he discovered the treachery—had accepted infidel blood money to hand him over. Good fortune or the will of Allah, though, had spared him the disgrace of capture, or worse. With funds accumulated from the bounty placed on the heads of Americans by former regime members in hiding, he bought safe passage to Syria. There, he found other warriors, among them officers and top officials who had been granted refuge by the Syrians. They had a plan, he learned. They were biding their time...

Zhabat suddenly noticed the black beret glaring, inquiring if he was boring him.

"Continue," Zhabat said, matching the infidel's scowl.

As further compensation, the Brazilian colonel, Turkle said, was storing a toxic cargo that would make any dirty bomb they could slap together seem like a firecracker in comparison. The Brazilian, he noted, was shifting from foot to foot, as if he'd been dumped on the hot seat. They would receive a portion of this special cargo as a gift, but only for successful services rendered. The prisoners were going to be freed, he heard, and flown to their countries of origin...eventually. When Zhabat lifted an eyebrow at that, Turkle told him there was one stop in Turkey before their release. And it involved what Zhabat already knew was smuggled out of his country before the infidels began raining their smart bombs on Baghdad. The American and his people wanted a large haul out of what was stashed in Turkey, were prepared to divvy it up, however, according to which side did how much of the dirty work to get it. No tricks, no trap, Turkle vowed. Ahabat figured if American Special Ops wanted him and his troops in the bag, they would have come through the front door already.

"What's your answer?" Turkle asked.

Zhabat decided to take his time before speaking. He unfolded his legs, leaned toward the coffee table and stabbed out his smoke. "I should seek counsel from my men before I give you an answer," he said.

"There's no time. In or out? Look, I read you as an up-and-comer in whatever organization you pledge allegiance to, Hamas, Hezbollah, the Warrior Sons of Islam, I don't care. Think about it. This could be a major coup for you and your troops. You free your own, see them home safely and you've got infidel scalps on your belts to show for yourselves. You'd be a hero."

Persuasive, Zhabat thought, and true. But there were other considerations, beyond selfish ambition. There were operations on the table, but they were still in the preliminary stages, months, if not a year or more away from being launched. Say he accepted, would it delay or even derail future operations, for which he had been sent to Paraguay to oversee? Then there were his brothers in captivity to consider, potentially to be freed at last to fight the infidel evil again, and all of whom would surely praise his name if he followed through with a successful attack on Camp Triangle. There was Turkey to factor in. He was aware of how valuable that special ordnance would prove in the fight against the occupiers if he could get his hands on, at worst, a small portion of it. Last and far from least, there was his own hatred of the infidels who had ravaged his country, killed, maimed, or captured and shamed his Sunni brothers and their leaders.

Zhabat decided he had seen far too many of his brothers in jihad slain by the infidels to let this opportunity to avenge their blood pass him by.

"Done," Zhabat answered.

Turkle looked around the room. "I was hoping for more than eight shooters."

"I have five more men nearby I can round up."

"Send a man, but have the others meet you," Turkle said. Zhabat didn't like the sound of that, watching carefully as the American produced a folded piece of paper and handed it to him.

"Directions to where you are to sit tight and wait for my return."

Zhabat chuckled.

"What's so funny?"

"I was thinking I would take you or the colonel with me," he said, watching Poscalar as he snapped him a startled look, "just in case, you understand, all does not go accordingly."

"No, I don't understand, and that's not happening. The two of us have some other business here in town before we make the big show. That's nonnegotiable."

Zhabat considered backing out, having both men shot where they stood. But, there was too much riding on this unusual deal. Perhaps, he decided, Allah was handing him a divine gift, unfurling a mysterious path where he could prove himself an invaluable, even holy asset to the coming victory of jihad.

"We'll do it your way," Zhabat said. "Now, I believe you mentioned something about money?" he added, watching as Turkle dug a thick wad of rubber-banded hundred-dollar bills from his jacket pocket.

He flipped it on the coffee table.

"That's fifty grand. Count it on your own time."

MUCH TO HIS SQUAD'S chagrin, Aurelio "the Zippo" Salvadore had sent the whores packing for the night, but with two ounces of snow just in from the lab and one hundred U.S. apiece in their pocketbooks for whatever time they felt they'd wasted. Granted, the gesture was pretty much show for the troops, in case the whores proved snippy about stopping by the next time they were called, and the blame for the inconvenience landed on his shoulders.

It was a tough job, he thought, keeping everybody happy.

Through the open door to his upstairs office, he heard one of his crew bark a vicious curse, the man no doubt folding another losing hand. If he thought about the moment the anger would rise like an invisible fire, from belly to brain, until no amount of whiskey or pure powder electrifying and sharpening his senses to superhuman limits cooled the flames. There he was, manning the phone, waiting for Colonel Poscalar's promised callback once he was inside the city, and his men couldn't stop indulging their whims and wants long enough to get their hearts and minds on business.

Exactly what job Poscalar had on tap for them, though, he couldn't or wouldn't say, and that only wound the wire tighter on his agitation and anxiety. Their commander had sounded strange on the phone, afraid perhaps, if he judged correctly the vague quiver he recalled in Poscalar's voice. Given what irons he knew were in the fire, he surmised Poscalar's anticipated visit had to do with either the latest shipment from the Bolivian traffickers or the mysterious cargo they were sitting on for the American colonel. Whichever it was, it involved money—primarily another man's—and Salvadore found himself wishing for simpler times.

Not to mention the hope of returning home to Rio, with his alleged crimes pardoned.

Another shot of whiskey down the hatch, another nose full of product huffed up through the sleek gold tube, and he palmed the television remote, easing back in his leather swivel chair. He snapped on the giant screen TV, hoping the porno flick would distract him from the gnawing paranoia that something was about to go terribly wrong. He considered storming out onto the catwalk to demand his crew stop playing with themselves, watch the damn store, inside and out. But he realized he would appear petty, denying them their simple pleasures while they rode out the wait for Poscalar.

And wasn't he just like them, even though he was second in command below Poscalar? A fugitive in hiding, a former military policeman of respect and prominence who had only been doing what was necessary to get ahead.

Cursing, quickly rewinding the lesbian scene, he sat up, chomped down on a Cuban cigar. He took up the ivory Zippo lighter, clacked the lid open and rolled the wheel. The flame leaped up before his eyes, large and dancing, orange with a sort of blue aura, he thought, so very beautiful to behold. Mesmerizing. The soft caress of a beautiful woman. Almost as if, yes, it was a living thing, calling him to use it on something, anything...anyone.

Precisely when he had fallen under the awe and rapture of fire was a memory he did not cherish. Feeling his cheeks flush hot with shame, he recalled tracking his wife to the seaside villa of her lover. So enraged and humiliated over the sight of their coupling, the idea had come out of nowhere, leaping into his thoughts, just like the fire he now stared into, as he touched it to the cigar tip, puffing slowly, working up a fat boiling cloud. At gunpoint, he remembered forcing her to tie up her lover, then binding her beside him. They lay together, they could die together. He emptied a five-gallon can of gasoline on and around the bed. A few last words delivered, a bitter eulogy, indeed, then he lit the soaking sheet with his Zippo lighter.

From that moment on, he came to understand the all-cleansing power and righteous fury of fire. Oh, but the first time, he recalled, had felt like a magical purifying rite of passage. It emboldened him with a vision he was destined to use fire, like a divine scourge, to rid Brazil of all its iniquities.

Salvadore noticed he was trembling. He told himself to calm down, focus, the future would take care of itself. He was drawing hard and deep on the cigar, one eye on the celluloid female coupling, his mind flaming with fantasies of what he wished to do the next time the whores trooped in when—

It felt like an eternity for the ungodly racket down on the warehouse floor to register in his mind for what it was. Gunfire, shouts of panic pounded through the doorway, the sum total of the din warning him they were being hit by a small armed force. But who? What bastards would dare attack them with such brazenness? They had jealous rivals in the city, to be certain. They were up-and-coming criminal rabble, he knew, having used several of them back east for tasks best suited for flunkies. They had transplanted their scroungy lot here from Rio and São Paulo, now seeking, if he heard correctly from informants, to cut their way into the Triangle's flourishing drug trade. But was this, what sounded a fullfrontal assault, the warrior style of what was essentially a pack of hyenas?

No, he decided, this was an attack by lions.

Salvadore was up, vaguely aware the cigar was falling from his gaping mouth, when the first explosion erupted. His mind screamed at him how absurd it was, how it was impossible for such a monstrous thing to be happening, as he felt the floor trembling beneath him, glimpsed the boiling smoke cloud beyond the door, the ragged figures sailing for the roof, the rising fifty-five-gallon drums looking warped and spewing their contents.

Insanity! The injustice of it all!

They were protected by the corrupt Paraguayan police, the greedy piranhas so heavily paid from drug money every week. They were ordered to not venture anywhere near the neighborhood, lest they felt they could make themselves too at home, pilfer merchandise, demand a bigger cut. No, the police wouldn't cut their own throats this way.

Salvadore froze when he heard the screams. They were hellish sounds he knew all too well from the ghosts of his own past, that piercing shriek when flesh was burned off bone, the screamer howling for death to end the agony. Another massive blast muted for a moment all that wailing, but he feared that earthshaker would not only bring the walls down but vaporize the Bolivian merchandise.

He was moving somehow, afraid to venture beyond the door, but he had to know, had to do something to save the night as he grabbed his assault rifle from the corner. Bounding onto the catwalk, two of his men sweeping by, weapons extended but ready to shoot at what he couldn't determine, he felt his knees buckle as he breathed in the stench. He nearly retched, as the vile unfamiliar odor that smelled of sulfuric acid and raw sewage but many times worse, assaulted his senses.

Horrified by what he saw next, Salvadore stood, watching as some green oily wave began falling over three of his men below. They were flailing about, clawing at their faces, thrashing on the floor next, with more drums thudding down, off the concrete floor, bouncing and splattering them with still more of the substance. Whatever it was, it acted like an invisible fire, consuming flesh, just the same. Salvadore thought he saw skin melting off their faces.

He heard his men firing downrange, turned, found them shooting down at the invaders, but who and how many was impossible to determine, as the smoke cloud boiled in that direction, providing cover for the enemy. The screams chilling him to the bone, Salvadore was moving to join his men, twenty paces and counting, when the catwalk vanished in a volcanic upheaval of fire and smoke. He was falling next, the gray world of smoke veiled by flying debris, wreckage slamming off his skull, white stars exploding in his eyes, but imploding back darkness at the same instant. He hammered the floor on his back, the air punched from his lungs, as he felt the sharp edges of raining trash pelt the length of his body. The screams, blessedly fading now—

Silence.

Slowly the faint but mounting crackle of fire penetrated his senses. He opened his eyes, wondering if he'd been knocked out and for how long, the abominable stench both wanting to revive but making him wish he was back in warm slumber. Gagging, he stared into the smoke, hoping his men had turned back the invaders, but feared, sensed the worst.

He thought he saw a tall dark shape coming his way, through the hazy wall of drifting smoke. Let it be one of his men, he hoped, as the figure seemed to glide closer, more like a floating wraith, as nausea swelled his belly, shadowy mist filled his eyes.

He was about to call out to the shadow, but something in the way the figure moved sounded a silent alarm. There was a big object in his hands, a shotgun, he thought, then firelight, most likely, winked off the fixed cylinders, still smoking. None of his men had access to a weapon like that.

"Who are you?" Salvadore croaked, fearful the knifing pain in his lower back meant it was broken. "Help me. I have money…name your price…just get me out of here."

Salvadore heard himself cry out loud, then silently railed at the madness and injustice of it all. He thought he was about to pass out, when the faceless shadow appeared to gather speed, then punched a massive handgun into full view as he surged clear of the smoke and told him, "You're finished."

14

He had been around the hard way. Thus, in his vast bloody experience, Braden knew that when a man believed the world was out to get him, the truth on that grim score wasn't far behind—double-timing it, in fact, to catch and grind him up.

These were the facts of life.

One thorn in his side, Durham, was suddenly making noise he might be forced to come partially clean with the President when Camp Triangle was abandoned, what with the bodies of fifteen Marines strewed all over the grounds, the killers—TFT traitors—in the wind.

Talk about shearing the scapegoat, Braden thought angrily.

The man with the big plan, he thought, safe on the sidelines for the time being, counting on, maybe secretly admiring the dragons who could burn up the other guys in a fiery battlefield spume of blood and guts. But it was always the cannon fodder who ended up holding the shit end of the stick. Why was that, he wondered, and why, did Durham feel he deserved salvation? Why should he be first in line?

Any way it was hacked, Braden knew he would have his neck in the noose within hours, he'd be one of the planet's most wanted scumbags. Durham would surely mix half-truths with bald-faced lies to cover his own assets while steering blame his way and urging the President to marshal a hunting expedition until he uncorked the genie for his own big event.

And then there was Compton. What a pain in the ass, Braden thought as the general intercepted him as soon as he stepped from the armory, bombarding him behind the foul winds of whiskey with the latest round of worry and fear, pointing at the Gulfstream as it lifted off for points unknown with Mohammed Bal-Ada in tow.

If nothing else, the general would be easy enough to reach out to and eliminate.

"I can see it," Braden snarled, wondering if he shouldn't just unsling his submachine gun and drop Compton, there and then. The guard towers were manned by his men, after all, part of the deadly plot about to see fruition, as soon as the hired guns from Ciudad del Este were in place, and Turkle and Hanover returned to lead the attack.

And then there was Stone, poised to drop the hammer on the place, he was sure, Compton railing on about how Washington surely knew by now they were running a Gestapo-style prison camp.

No question, their number was up.

"I don't like this, Colonel. What we're about to do is an abomination, sacrilege, you want the truth, to the uniform! What kind of soldier are you? Killing Arab fanatics, the dung of the earth who murder the innocent is one thing, but you're prepared to murder United States Marines, young guys, most of them, husbands and fathers, for God's sake." Compton was sounding hysterical.

"General, trust me, when I tell you God wants nothing to do with us. Nothing at all," Braden said.

He suspected it was all really beyond hope. Standing there, ready to sink in a pity pot maybe, infected by Compton's weakness of spirit, he figured himself ignored, at best, abandoned at worst by God, country and CENTCOM.

Compton cried out, "You kill Marines, it's a sure death sentence for all of us—"

"Only if we're caught, General." Braden chuckled, wondered if the future would prove as bleak and horrible as the past. Could he stand again on his own and kick the seemingly insurmountable demons of the present in the teeth? What choice did he have? "Where we're headed, as of tonight, we will be surrounded and protected by fighting men of like thinking and standing. Pull yourself together, General, you knew what was going to happen here. You chose this, even if you think someone else chose it for you. You made some bad choices along the way. You know we will be covered, new identities," he said, lifting the war bag stuffed with spare clips, grenades, C-4 and remote detonators and three hundred thousand in cash, "with a bag full of money."

"I forgot . You have all the answers."

Braden felt his anger intensify, but for once didn't erupt. No, he didn't have any answers, other than to bail, grab whatever good the future held for him. Had he possessed all the right answers, he wouldn't be here now. Briefly, he wondered if maybe he wasn't punishing himself for the lives of young Green Berets snuffed out in Afghanistan. Had he folded his hand following that debacle? Was becoming one of history's worst traitors a form of suicide by itself, leaving behind a legacy of shame? Even though, if cornered, he was ready to go out with a roar, was there still a part of him that was…

A coward?

Would living right, with honor, be the best revenge? He knew things were too far gone to stop what was already on the way.

And what was about to happen.

Fifteen United States Marines would be served up by his hand. And for what?

Braden squared his shoulders. "It's a little late in the game, General, to grow a conscience. And need I remind you, sir, that you are bought and paid for. If you want to step off I have all your sins and crimes documented and ready to dump off on CENTCOM. Now, if you'll excuse me, I have a lot of work to do," Braden said, brushing past Compton, thinking if he stood there any longer he would eliminate his first problem on impulse.

"It's murder, Braden," Compton shouted.

Braden clenched his teeth, felt sick to his stomach. "No. It's the first step to freedom," he said, hating himself as soon as the words left his mouth.

Freedom? he wondered, thinking he chuckled with a bitterness best reserved for an adder swallowing its own venom.

Freedom from what?

15

The Executioner knew the clock was ticking. Already the southern portion of the city was jumping with sirens and teeming with local authorities. From there on, he needed to pick up the pace, Michaels having guided him swiftly to round two, some five blocks north from the Brazilian death squad's abattoir.

Bolan got lucky, as far as breaching the terror nest went. The terrorist in question was at the front door to the apartment, knocking, there, Bolan figured, to beef up an armed contingent his eyes in the sky informed him was en route for Camp Triangle. Between the grim, nagging suspicion and the high-tech eavesdropping, Bolan believed Task Force Talon's top lieutenants and Poscalar were trying to hire shooters to besiege and lay waste to Camp Triangle. They could scratch Aurelio Salvadore and his murdering brigands from the lineup.

Bolan's gut warned him he had been followed into the building, and he had a good idea just who was tracking him. He checked the gloomy hall that reeked of stale urine, cigarette and marijuana smoke, and saw he was clear. The mini-Uzi with sound suppressor was snaking out from one of the deeper wells of his trenchcoat, tracking the terrorist just as the door opened. A bearded, swarthy man with pistol in hand was framed inside the jamb.

Who and how many armed combatants were inside Bolan couldn't say. He hated running blind, he knew the final outcome of any shooting engagement was usually only as good as the intelligence, but there was no choice.

Hit and run.

They came alive, all anger and fear at the sight of the Executioner's weapon, the guest digging inside his leather jacket, arming himself with a .44 Magnum pistol.

The Executioner held back on the compact weapon's trigger, stuttering forth a burst that zipped guest across the back first, then swept the host with a burst of 9 mm Parabellum rounds to the chest, leaving no doubt a grim reaper was onsite. Sudden vicious impact then gravity took over, guest folding into host, bodies collapsing inside the door in a sprawled tangle.

Bolan bounded over the bodies, taking in the trio in the spacious living room, when he sensed it all poised to go south. On the fly, attempting to grab temporary cover behind a belly-high-partitioned counter that separated the kitchen from living room, Bolan hit the mini-Uzi's trigger. The men were already in flight, two HK 33s and a submachine gun of indeterminate make blazing away, as they rolled over a large couch, out of sight but raging in Arabic, blasting wild. Bolan took in the hallway that fanned away to his three o'clock, wondering if the rooms held any lethal surprises. He had to believe they would have showed their hand by this time, which would mean a whole other world of hurt if they were riding out a few more seconds.

Bolan backed up against a fat pillar as the trio began spraying his cover, the tempest of lead blowing past, exploding cabinets, detonating glass, thudding a drumbeat across a refrigerator.

He was pinned.

Bolan charged low beneath the counter, rounds scream-

ing off the top, wood slivers and stucco blasting in minidet-
onations, biting at his nape, clawing at his cheeks before he
reached a moment's sanctuary behind the other pillar. He was
in the process of reaching for a frag grenade to end it when
the door behind him exploded in a thunderous eruption of
wood. A howl of pure rage, like that of a wild beast embroiled
in a savage contest, bellowed in his ears.

Bolan was wheeling in a one-eighty toward the threat
when the mini-Uzi was slapped from his hand and out into
the living room.

CONSIDERING HIMSELF a stone-cold professional, proud he
never lost control of his emotions no matter what the pressure cooker, Steven Turkle nonetheless struggled to maintain
a rapidly deteriorating composure. Between the snarled traffic slowing the GMC to a near crawl—when they were a mere
three blocks from rounding up the next group of shooters—
the mysterious but clearly horrific event he was attempting
to put behind in the southeast quarter of the city and Poscalar unraveling at the bad news he was receiving on the other
end of the cell phone transmission, it was all he could do to
cap his anger.

Clenching his jaw at Poscalar's bleating and whimpering,
Turkle suddenly imagined he heard his shouldered M-9 calling the man's name. Poscalar, he glimpsed, disgusted, was
rubbing his face, hanging his head, and damn near looked set
to break out in tears.

"Oh, God, no! All of it? No, no, no." Poscalar choked
down a sob, then found his former shadow of arrogance as
he launched the blame game. "Damn your eyes, Captain
Hoessvalez. I have paid you and all of your men promptly,
exorbitant sums, for protection, and compared to your paltry annual salaries you were meant to not only kiss the
ground on which I walk, but you were to make certain just

such a thing as what I'm hearing about never happens! Now you tell me my merchandise was melted? Six hundred kilos are now a steaming puddle of green slime? What do you mean you can't explain it? Whatever was in those drums—"

Turkle listened intently, still silently cursing traffic but closer to where he needed to be. It sounded like their cargo was history, either demolished or spilled in the attack. Whatever remained was likely to be seized by the Paraguayan authorities.

They were finished in South America, no question. And there would be no bartering their toxic haul. All the risk, the wasted effort, Turkle thought, to not only brew the toxin— created in a fly-by-night factory—but establish pipelines for potential buyers—

If it was true misery loved company, then Turkle found himself wanting to laugh out loud as Poscalar continued yelling into the cell phone.

"Your inefficiency on that is not my concern. I don't care about your lack of HAZMAT teams or that the building is quarantined. What troubles me is that you sound to be standing around, wringing your balls, which I will have mounted! Wrap a bandanna around your nose, for all I care, but get in there and double-check my merchandise…

"Of course, I want to know who did this, but you're telling there are no witnesses, other than a vagrant drunk," the Brazilian continued, after pausing to listen to his contact.

Whatever had happened to Poscalar's hired killers, Turkle surmised they had gone the way of the Bolivians' cocaine. The way he overheard it, the building was on fire, Poscalar's death squad fugitives littering the warehouse floor, fumes from within so overpowering no one could enter without donning a spacesuit. As evidenced by the sky over the low-lying neo-colonial structures behind, dancing in a swirling light show, Turkle knew all available law enforcement and military personnel would be scrambling in that direction.

Oh, well, he thought, so their shooting herd was thinned out. He hadn't put much stock in the warring capabilities of men who hunted down unarmed urchins in the streets of Rio anyway, who never put their lives on the firing line unless they were backed by overwhelming numbers and firepower. Poscalar's not-so-wild bunch, he concluded, had obviously come up against a warrior-sized predicament, and failed to cut it.

Traffic began jerking, car by car, toward the intersection, but Turkle spied a couple in the vehicle ahead, necking in the front seat. He laid on the horn.

Poscalar shrieked at him. Turkle growled back a curse.

"Impossible, Captain!" Poscalar shouted, eyes darting like a cornered animal. "They were thirteen trained professionals! And you're telling me your one witness 'believes' he saw one man leave the premises? Now you want to tell me ghost stories how one faceless marauder is responsible—"

Turkle chuckled and glimpsed Poscalar glaring at him with murderous wrath. He wasn't about to tell Poscalar his theory on the culprit, lest he was drawn into a long, bitter and fruitless argument, but Hanover had trailed Colonel Stone to the death squad compound, and his eyewitness account about who walked out with smoke and leaping flames in his wake was believable, albeit incredible.

There was suspicion, though, from the moment they'd laid on eyes on Washington's man. Turkle knew that Stone was way more than just a DOD or Pentagon desk-lifer, sent to Camp Triangle to fill out paperwork in triplicate for his superiors.

In a way, it made their job that much easier—Washington looking to hide the truth from the public, cover its own shame over an operation and a base that painted them borderline outlaw—that Stone was black ops. The coming war would serve as both a graveyard for the unwelcomed and a giant smoke screen, both meant to hurl up enough confusion and mystery until they were at least halfway across the Atlantic. Or so went Braden's plan.

As he heard Poscalar groan, dumping the cell phone on the floorboards, he caught a break at the intersection. With just enough room to zip between a tour bus and another vehicle, Poscalar screaming about the sudden jolt, Turkle lurched them into a dark gap between two shops and shut the GMC down.

Poscalar looked on the verge of puking, as he said, "I am holding Braden personally responsible for my loss. He should have told me how volatile that cargo was. Why didn't he tell me it was a substance like sulfuric acid? I would never—do you realize how much money I have lost—no, how much money I owe the Bolivians? That shipment was only partly paid for! It was on consignment, good faith. Millions…perhaps tens of millions—"

Turkle reached over the seat and hauled up his war bag, then gathered the nylon satchel beneath his legs. When Poscalar dropped his face in his hands, whimpering, Turkle whipped out the M-9 and jammed the muzzle in the man's ear.

Poscalar slowly pulled his face out of his hands, eyes bulging. "Wh-what…are you doing?"

"You pull it together now, Colonel, or I will drop you right here. Your scumbags with badges are dead, your coke is gone, but so is our cargo, which, by the way, I don't hear you crying all that much about. Are you going to follow through in helping me scrounge up this riffraff for what I—no we—have to do? Think hard before you answer. You still have a world to save—as in your own life."

Poscalar seemed to calm down, considering something,

lips flapping but no sound emerging for several moments. "Very well. Perhaps…perhaps all is not lost."

Whatever that meant, Turkle guessed the Brazilian's mind was tumbling with an avalanche of excuses, rationales for the Bolivians, or how he would divert the blame for his disaster. It didn't matter. He already knew Poscalar's ultimate fate.

"Fall out," Turkle said, opening his door as he stowed the M-9.

BEFORE CRASHING THE GATE, Bolan knew the play was dicey. He had next to zero intelligence on numbers, layout, type and how many weapons, no positive ID and background on the players. He had no idea if his move was a straight bullrush, where he should have drawn first blood. There was no contingency plan in the event of unforeseen disaster, no concrete or even vague mental sketch for an escape hatch.

He grappled with his attacker, his throat being squeezed so hard he felt like his eyeballs were ready to pop from their sockets. Bolan knew he had but two heartbeats, tops, to turn the tide. A foot stomp, a knee to the groin was out of the question. Only a crippling blow to his human vise would unclamp his throat.

Locked in a near slow dance step with his adversary, the Executioner somehow slid his left arm across his body, a tight tunneling motion between two walls of flesh, before he clawed at his right hip and slid the Desert Eagle free. He jerked his own feet back, as far as he could, the spittle and snarling rage of his opponent in his face. He figured he had the mammoth handgun on-line, and squeezed the trigger. There was a sonic boom, followed a microsecond later by a roar of agony.

Not a second to spare, as the man toppled into the kitchen, bringing down a rack of pots and pans, the Executioner flung himself around the edge of the pillar, free hand coming around, filled with the Beretta. It was impossible to say how much time had elapsed—most likely four to six seconds—but the trio of terrorists had apparently opted to sit tight, leave the problem to fate.

Fatal mistake.

The Executioner tapped the Desert Eagle's trigger, catching one midvault over the couch, a crimson bull's-eye erupting through the sternum. The man was hurtled backward with the mule-kick impact into crimson mist, assault rifle flying from his hands and hammering the wall as Bolan tracked on, double-tapping the triggers on both weapons. The second target was howling, one hand swiping at blood in his eyes, when Bolan tagged him with a round each from Beretta and Desert Eagle. The terrorist was lifted off his feet from near point-blank double impact before landing in a heap, twitching out beside his fallen comrade. The third man swept a burst in Bolan's general direction, but it was powered most likely by panic, as rounds tattooed the far pillar from the Executioner. Three went to ground again as Bolan blasted out another pair of rounds.

But Bolan still had lethal problems, front and back. One hunkered behind the sofa, prolonging the standoff, another adversary growling and cursing to get back into the fray.

A flashing look down the hall showed clear, and Bolan pivoted toward the shouting man, Beretta drawing a bead between his eyes as he wobbled, hand braced against a counter. The Executioner painted a 9 mm dead-eye in his forehead.

Then another hostile reared up, out of nowhere.

Bolan was turning death sights toward the couch when he glimpsed a dark and armed shape floating across the front door. The soldier's hearing was cut to near deafness by the din of close quarters combat, but his eyes and combat instinct picked up the slack.

There was no mistaking the black beret with the screaming hawk, as Hanover grabbed a knee beside the front door and cut loose with his submachine gun.

16

It was a proud moment for Solano Fulgenzial when his two expected guests stepped through the front door. For once, a man of notoriety, of power and means needed him.

During the hours after he received the first call from the Brazilian colonel, he had pondered the immediate future—namely his own.

The colonel needed ten to twelve hired guns for an as yet unspecified job. Fulgenzial was not personally acquainted with the man, who was rumored to have headed numerous death squads in Rio de Janeiro, but he had, on occasion, been hired out by the Colonel's underlings. He knew they were holed up in the southern part of the city, dealing large quantities of narcotics, reaping illicit profits he had, up to now, only dreamed of.

The payment for torching an abandoned building of squatters in Rio, or executing a drug dealer unwilling to pay tribute back then seemed insulting compared to what he was being promised.

Was this opportunity to be a turning point in his life? he wondered. His time to shine?

As the whiskey flowed and the lines of coke were huffed up, a few of the angrier members of his gang began fiddling with their assault rifles, spouting bluster about whose blood they hoped they would be hired to shed. He already knew the answer, even without concrete specifics from the colonel's end.

Crime did pay, he thought, whether in São Paulo, Rio or Ciudad del Este, but the choice meat always went to the hungrier predator always ready and willing to act with indiscriminate ferocity to feed himself. It made no difference who or what he consumed with violence, as long his belly—his wallet—was fat. And, in both Brazil and Paraguay, there was plenty of prey, opportunity forever calling to those unafraid to dip their hands in blood. The problem facing him, though, was how to climb the ladder to the success he so desired. There were any number of crime cartels operating out of the Triangle, and they alone were proving a stumbling block to group and personal ambitions. From the Japanese Yakuza, the Russian mafiya, la Cosa Nostra, to the Nigerian heroin gangs looking to set up shop here, they all carried the briefcases stuffed with cash, wielded the latest in technology and firepower, and had command and control of all the right contacts.

For some time he had been looking to cut himself into the cocaine trade. He was tired of running whores, strong-arming local shopkeepers, stealing cars, or dabbling in small arms sales that earned little more than a good three- or four-day bender. Fulgenzial knew he needed a lucky break, just one, and he would be on his way to greater things. Money first, then power and respect. He had some ideas in that regard, and the future, suddenly looking bright and promising, was heading right his way.

As he eased back in his chair at the round table in the cantina of the gang's clubhouse, Fulgenzial ran a hand over his bristled scalp. He was watching, sizing up his guests as, flanked by two gang members with Russian AKMs, they slowly traversed the short foyer.

Though they were around the corner, off the main drag of the hotel block, and tucked midway down a row of shops and boutiques—recently abandoned for failure to pay tribute to the new alliance—Fulgenzial found it somewhat strange the normal pulse of party nightlife was not up to thundering levels. One of his men looked out the door, checking the alley in both directions. Moments later, Fulgenzial saw him throw a curt nod, giving both himself and the man to his right side the all-clear.

The gangster poured another shot of whiskey and glanced through the smoke cloud at his co-leader, Paulo Santival. Like the other ten members of his crew, Santival wore a new red beret with skull and crossbones insignia. A 9 mm Makarov pistol was displayed in a shoulder holster where he let his leather jacket hang open and loose. Santival was known for intimidating first impressions and had a vicious reputation that backed him up. A killer, whose lily-white hands had been immersed in the blood of whole neighborhoods in Rio's slums, Santival kept his AKM across his lap.

Fulgenzial watched as the colonel and the Yankee with the two nylon bags approached. Both of them, he observed, took in his armed force, scattered down the length of the bar, twenty strong under the roof. The colonel, Fulgenzial thought, looked pale, as if set to collapse from illness, his eyes glazed. The nameless Yankee in the black beret ran a contemptuous look around the squalid interior, his tongue clucking in disapproval.

Fulgenzial smiled at the colonel. This was his turf, their terms would be met, but Fulgenzial felt anger stir the longer the Yankee eyeballed him like he was nothing more than a bug.

"Let's do this," the American said.

"And you are?" Fulgenzial asked.

"Your temporary boss."

Fulgenzial glanced at Santival, who appeared more interested in the Colonel. "Colonel Poscalar. It's been awhile. I have to say, you don't look so good."

"He just got some bad news," the Yankee said, "regarding a few family members."

Santival arched an eyebrow, grinning, blowing smoke their way. "Really? My condolences."

Fulgenzial wondered if it was a croak or a sob he heard as he saw the colonel teetering. But the Yankee launched into what he wanted them to do, barking orders, before he could decide. At first, Fulgenzial thought the plan was either suicidal, or they were being set up by Brazilian authorities working in collusion with Americans. The Yankee assured him it was a straight hit, no tricks, no ambush, as if reading his thoughts. They were to kill anyone in uniform who didn't wear black with the matching beret. Why, the Yankee didn't explain, but there was an armory inside the prison fence, packed with the latest in military hardware, and they could help themselves to the whole store, if they agreed, if they did the job. Their team would follow the Yankee to an undisclosed location and move only on his orders.

Fulgenzial looked at Santival, the man's face betraying no expression. Santival met his eye.

"We can spare you twelve men," Santival said.

"But the price is four thousand per shooter," Fulgenzial added, in negotiating lockstep with his partner, both of them having hashed out their conditions beforehand.

"With an extra ten thousand thrown in," Santival said, "for the pleasure of their company."

As the Yankee snorted and delved into his windbreaker, he said, "Then they better damn well understand I'm paying for more than just some bullshit joyride."

"They do," Santival said.

The Yankee was dropping six rubber-banded bundles of U.S. hundreds on the table when Fulgenzial said, "One more thing."

The Yankee bared his teeth. "That's sixty grand. There is no more."

"It doesn't involve any more of your money," Fulgenzial said.

"What?"

"We have an interest in breaking into new business ventures," Santival said. "Despite what you might think, we are not a bunch of neo-Nazi scum, living in the past."

"The colonel stays here with us," Fulgenzial said.

From where the Executioner stood, with nowhere to bolt for cover without getting cut to ribbons in the attempt. There was no lesser of two evils. It was small comfort in the heat of the moment, but the gray area blurring the picture before then was obliterated. Bolan knew Braden and his brigands were fair game, assuming he made it out of there alive.

With the latest tempest blowing over his scalp and whizzing past an ear in a hot rush of hair trimming, Bolan lurched behind the pillar, out of Hanover's line of fire, but exposed to his other adversary. The last terrorist standing, though, didn't appear too eager to jump back into the fray. The lack of nerves or something else altogether granting Bolan a critical heartbeat or two of grim respite. Either way, there was no option, he knew, but stand hard, keep blazing.

One eye on the living room, Bolan drove Hanover to cover around his doorjamb post with a double Beretta–Desert Eagle blast, then spied the subgun's muzzle, peeking up, midway down the couch.

A half-pivot, and the Executioner unloaded the mammoth Desert Eagle where he framed the invisible target to mind. Two blasts, and Bolan blew a gaping tunnel through fabric. Stuffing spumed into the misty scarlet hitting the air as a howl of pain competed for Hanover's return engagement, a head popping into Bolan's view.

Between the spray and pray of the terrorist shuddering to his feet, pounding out a subgun burst with what appeared to be his only good arm and Hanover's cold professional comeback, Bolan nearly bought it. He hit the deck, rounds tattooing the hallway cornerstone, thrust the Beretta around the gnawed edge and capped off rounds. The 9 mm peppering was flaying the doorjamb. Hanover was grunting and throwing himself out of sight, when Bolan lifted the Desert Eagle and dropped the terrorist with a .44 Magnum round through the chest. A fresh spray stained white stucco already streaked with running blood and chewed bits of flesh and cloth, the terrorist crash-landed, down and out.

One man left. Or so Bolan hoped, as he found the Beretta's slide locked open. He quickly changing clips on both weapons.

"Stone! Listen to me! It doesn't have to be like this!" Hanover shouted.

Ears ringing, straining to catch the words, Bolan raised himself to a knee, peered around the pillar.

"That was some sweet work you did on Poscalar's bunch!"

The Executioner stowed the Desert Eagle. He was way overdue bailing, he knew, as he dug into a pocket, palmed a frag grenade and pulled the pin.

"I'll put in a good word for you. Braden could use a man of your obvious talent. Camp Triangle's going up in flames, Stone. It's over. Washington can go to hell, truth is, it's going to anyway. There's big stakes once we blow the Triangle, but big reward for anybody with the program! You listening, Stone?" Hanover called out.

Bolan sounded a grim chuckle, released the spoon, set it silently on the floor. Beretta blasting at the jamb, he rolled the steel egg, bowling it toward the corpses wedged in the opening. He was up and sprinting down the hall, glancing back as Hanover surged into the doorway, HK subgun stuttering. Bolan felt rounds punch through where his coat flowed out like an umbrella, as he flung himself into a nosedive. There was abrupt silence, as he belly flopped, sliding on for deeper cover down the hall, wrapping arms around his head. He thought he heard Hanover shouting a curse, a milisecond before the expected thunderclap.

Rising, Beretta aimed at the smoke boiling down the hall, Bolan retraced his path. Senses choked, rolling into the foul vapor, and he found what was left of Hanover was little more than bug splatter, from foyer all the way across the hall.

There was another blitz to go in the heart of one of the world's most notorious criminal havens before he'd be on his way to what would become yet another raging hell, if the words from the late and unlamented Hanover held even a ring of truth. Regrettable, to some extent, as he knew there was plenty of butcher's work needed in Ciudad del Este.

Maybe another day, assuming there was a future beyond this night.

Retrieving his mini-Uzi, the warrior was all adrenaline and steam as he beat a hard march toward his exit. Mini-Uzi and Beretta leading the way, he bulled through the jagged shards where his first attacker had come through the door and body-slammed him to the pillar with such force and rung his neck so hard.

No time to nurse a few battered muscles and sore ribs, even if he was so inclined. He made a rolling weapons sweep of the tiny bedroom, a check under the bed and closet, but finding no snakes ready to bite at his heels, he headed for the window, which was barred inside with an iron grate. He shot the lock off with a 3-round burst.

The job was far from over, the worst, he suspected, yet to come, but Bolan nodded as he spotted the roof of his GMC directly below. A straight drop, figure less than twenty feet to the vehicle's roof, and Bolan went for it.

18

"Take it easy on the booze, big man. The three of us need to talk business. I want straight talk, straight answers, not a bunch of promises you'll forget when the hangover wears off tomorrow."

Hunched and staring into the shotglass, Poscalar ignored the skinhead.

The overpowering urge to crack up into a weeping fit had ebbed to black depression after the first two drinks. Now, with half the bottle of cheap tequila burning his belly, Poscalar felt a dangerous fire spreading, loosening limbs, shooting wild and crazy thoughts through his mind. Desperate men, he knew, could prove reckless to the extreme, the most dangerous and cunning animals alive, truth be told. Nothing left to lose, take as many along the way before checking out, sure as there was fire in hell, he thought. Was he of that lion pride? Or was there something to hope for—any reason left to live?

Either way, he wasn't sure he could control himself much longer, as he glanced at the AKM assault rifle at the end of the bar, three stools down, unattended. The other thugs, he noted, looking quickly into the bar mirror, were busy swilling from bottles, snorting lines. His world had all but shattered, and it incensed him they were whooping it up, this vicious racist trash who had never known a real dollar in their sorry lives, as they slapped cash on a big table in the far corner, cheering for or cursing whoever they were betting their night's earnings on over a game of cards.

Shock effect had thankfully begun wearing off, the nausea no longer threatening to see him faint, silent hysteria having faded to cold anger once the henchman abandoned him to the gang of thugs. Briefly, Poscalar hated himself, recalling how meekly he had submitted to their demand he remain, pretty much a prisoner, and one on death row if any number of disasters flew back in his face. How could it get any worse? He went straight for the bottle, shoving the shot glass away with the back of his hand.

"What's wrong with you, Colonel? You look like a man who has more than family problems. You look sick. Please, do not puke all over my bar."

The colonel choked down the bitter curse, as the rabble took a stool, one on either side. Chugging from the bottle, he considered confessing the truth. They were small fish looking to morph themselves into rich man-eaters. His fear was that the truth would most definitely get him killed on the spot. He knew Santival from Rio, and the man's reputation for getting what he wanted, whatever it took, made Poscalar think carefully about how to proceed. Despite the night's horror and the frightening uncertainty of the immediate future, the dark thoughts faded as he knew, deep in his heart, he wanted to keep breathing. With luck, some fast talking and slapping together a few million here, a few million there from various accounts he had scattered from Rio to the Caymans, he might appease the Bolivians. He would direct the blame toward the corrupt, bungling Paraguayan police he had paid great personal sums to for protection. The vengeful wrath of the Bolivians would be fearsome and swift.

"Colonel, I get the impression you are either ignoring us, or you don't care too much for us," Fulgenzial said.

"How very perceptive of you."

Santival, he saw, started to scowl, then erupted in laughter. "That's much better. Now, that's the mean-spirited bastard of Rio I used to know."

Poscalar grunted, pulled away from the bottle. "So, you want to be big-shot traffickers, Scarface."

Fulgenzial spoke up. "We'd settle for something more in the midlevel distribution range."

Santival clapped Poscalar on the back. "Enough so we can get out of this dump, maybe drive a new sports car."

"We're not the flashy types," Fulgenzial said. "We don't want the world."

"Just a small corner of it. We kind of like it here in Ciudad del Este. But we need to make money, good money. Whatever else follows, some fame, women, respect and honor…" Santial grinned.

"We're certain you have surplus on hand," Fulgenzial said.

The wheels were spinning in Poscalar's head. "This would all hinge on how much you want, how much cash you can come up with."

Santival put an edge to his voice. "And that is all hinging, Colonel, on how our men fare tonight. How many return. How much of this hardware we receive as bonus."

"Meaning," Fulgenzial added, "if the Yankee lives up to his arrogant words."

Poscalar hoped he kept a straight face. He looked in the mirror, spotting the white pile on their table. "Do you mind if I go to your table and help myself to a little inspiration on that note?"

"Go crazy," Santival said.

"We'll still be here," Fulgenzial said, and chuckled. "Waiting on good news about the future between us."

Poscalar took the bottle, stood on legs fortified by tequila and felt the eyes on him in the mirror as he went to the table.

Was all hope truly lost? he wondered, the din of buzzed and intoxicated bedlam fading in his ears suddenly as he felt the dark mood wanting to take hold once more. The American, he greatly suspected, was not coming back. And Braden and the useless General Compton were in the process of putting Brazil behind them.

Then what? How to salvage whatever was left of the future?

There was a chance, a slim one, granted, he could pry— more like con—a decent chunk of cash from the rabble. With that, he could pad his own money, seek out another trafficker in the Triangle for the time being, deal enough on his own to further gain ground on what he owed the Bolivians.

Hope, indeed, there was a chance he could redeem himself, save his world, keep building the dream.

He sat at the table, feeling better about the prospects of the future—perhaps it was time, after all, to form a new alliance. He was lifting the tube when he saw a tall dark figure walk through the front door. It took two heartbeats for Poscalar to determine the big man in the black leather trench coat didn't belong there, and that he was a clear and present menace.

He heard the rabble shouting at the stranger to identify himself. They were coming unglued at the bar, when the nameless shadow showed his right arm, hauling the assault rifle with fixed grenade launcher out from under the cover of his left coat flap. Poscalar felt his eyes bug, jaw slack, his sphincter twitch as he watched the big stranger blow the rabble off their stools with a burst of autofire that sent them flying, crashing to the floor in a bloody heap.

Men were screaming, cursing up a storm, trying to haul out their weapons, when the stranger shifted his aim, the rocket launcher chugging. It was all Poscalar could do to keep from vomiting, as he flung himself to the floor, the missile streaking overhead, sailing on. He threw his arms over his head, held on, eating grimy floorboard. The explosion rocked his world. As rubble and bits and pieces of wet flesh rained down on the length of his body, it was next to impossible to discern if those were shouts of rage or screams of men shredded by the blast. He looked out. The stranger was cutting loose with the assault rifle, marching on, column to post, into the smoke. Poscalar couldn't believe what he watched. The stranger was gunning down anyone left standing in the smoke.

It was more than Poscalar could bear. The Bolivians' coke going up in smoke—or reduced to a pool of green slime— paled in comparison to the notion he was moments away from being executed. It was time to take matters into his own hands.

Poscalar was scrabbling across the floor on hands and knees, the AKM laying at the foot of the stool, growing larger, but still seeming a mile away. One by one they stopped screaming, bodies crashing across the room. He listened to the silence, thought he heard a scraping sound, saw the stranger—or the shadow of the man as it melted deeper into the drifting pall. He flinched, hating the startled cry that tore out of his mouth when he heard the 3-round stutter sealing the tomb on some wounded gangster's moaning.

He hauled in the AKM, wobbling to his feet, searching the smoke. "Whoever you are, listen to me! I am rich! I will pay you to let me walk out of here! This garbage here, they meant nothing to me! I do not hold you responsible! As far as I am concerned, you just made the world a better place!"

Crouching, he darted down the bar, fell in behind a partition. Scouring the smoke, he cursed, then wondered if maybe the stranger had walked out. Another hideous groan sounded, followed by another brief stammer of weapons fire. Poscalar popped up, AKM sweeping the litter of bodies. "Answer me, damn you!" he shouted.

He was listening to the thunder of his heart in his ears, panning on, when the big shadow fell out from behind a column. Poscalar was torn between throwing his weapon away or shooting when the stranger made the decision for him. As the colonel felt the bullets tearing into his chest, driving him into the bar, his dying thought was how terribly unjust it was.

19

"We're on. Check and set. Ten seconds starting now."

When all hands copied over the com link, Braden hung the nylon bag over his shoulder. He marched out of the comm center, the last of the C-4 blocks fixed to Compton's crotch—the gruesome coup de grâce to bringing down the roof. He figured it would take a team of forensic specialists days before they had enough of the man scraped up on a petri dish for a DNA sample, and by then they would have either wrapped up the overseas part of the operation, or Washington, D.C., would be a glowing speck.

Or all of them would be dead.

Braden didn't even give the general's sprawled body a last look. Compton had cracked, bottom line, the last vestiges of whatever honor in uniform he thought he owned getting the better of him. He was going to call Washington himself, he had reached for his weapon....

Screw him.

Braden had fifteen armed problems to contend with at the moment. And since he hadn't been able to reach Hanover for a Stone sitrep he feared one more headache was on the way back.

Braden palmed the remote detonator.

Four, three...

Thumbed on the red light. He'd rounded the corner when he heard the first retorts of weapons fire echoing his way.

Game time.

He hit the button, heard the thunder peal, sealing the tomb on the late and unlamented General Compton, and kept on marching into the future.

ZHABAT WAS NOT ENTIRELY convinced the infidels were playing it straight. There was one dead Marine in the guard booth at the west gate, but Zhabat wasn't about to let his guard down. Defying the order for radio silence, he had attempted to call the second group while waiting for the signal. No answer meant something had gone wrong, but what? If they were being marched into an ambush...

Zhabat looked at the Marine, wondering which part he should take as a trophy, was sliding his knife free when a voice snarled in his ear, "You don't want to do what you're thinking. Trust me."

Something warned Zhabat right then it might be best to turn around, retrace the half-mile hike back to the trail where their vehicles were parked. This felt all wrong. He put the knife back in its scabbard, angry that he was being put in his place in front of his men.

"Move it out!" the black beret ordered, holding back until Zhabat waved his men past, then fell in.

Assault rifle in hand, Zhabat checked the wide open ground around and beyond the prison fence. East, he spotted the black transport plane, heard the turboprop engines firing up as it lumbered out from the hangar. A harder search of the hangar showed the string of tanker trucks and fuel bins, but no executive jet. At the last minute, though, the black beret had changed the orders. They were to storm the front gate. It was open. Closing hard, he made out the faint but growing rattle of autofire.

He was jogging for the opening, then slowed the pace, allowing his men to gain some distance when a group of four

Marines broke through a door in the prison. The Americans were moving to intercept the invaders, he knew, but suddenly faltered, turning back to the sound of weapons fire, shouting into handheld radios. Two more armed figures emerged from the lit doorway, and began spraying the Marines with a storm of fire.

THE EXECUTIONER WAS gripped by cold terrible anger, aware of what was happening inside the prison walls, and why.

He was back in combat harness and webbing, the Blaster 61 stuffed with a mix of HE and incendiary rounds, slung across his right shoulder. From the gunship's hatchway, as Michaels sailed them on a north to south vector, he took in the shock troops. Two groups were charging the prison walls on either side, each squad led by what appeared two Task Force Talon brigands, their weapons flaming away.

And they were all gunning down any Marines who ventured beyond the open doors.

Beyond treason, Braden was committing mass murder, having created the appearance of an assault on the compound by two different groups of killers he had hired from Ciudad del Este.

Smoke screen, Bolan knew, for his planned overseas flight. He was certain Task Force Talon and its paymasters had more than just one iron in the fire, as he recalled Hanover's vow that Washington was going to burn.

Bolan wasn't about to mentally kick himself for losing time on the last round of the Ciudad del Este kill parade. Braden thought himself clever, he was sure, sticking Hanover to his six while rustling up a cutthroat army to do his dirty work. To have allowed Poscalar to live to corrupt another day, to let the hired vermin go on perpetrating crimes against decent citizens would have galled him to no end. In the terms of cold logic that the only good venomous snake was a dead one, Bolan had eliminated a group of vipers who lived to serve only their own criminal interests and act out murderous impulses.

A plan quickly taking shape in the ice-cold resolve of lethal intent, Bolan keyed his com link and told Michaels what to do.

As the Stony Man blacksuit swung them out over a fenced arena inside the southern prison gate that Bolan assumed was the prison yard, he took in the firefight going full-tilt between Marines hunkered inside a doorway and a group of twelve or thirteen invaders.

Judging the leather jackets, AKMs and a smattering of red berets, Bolan decided to begin his bloody quest by savaging a few of Poscalar's thugs. The Marines had their firepoint inside the doorway dug in, their M-16s hosing the yard. Several of the thugs were spinning, weapons flying. It should have proved no match, trained professionals against criminal rabble, but one of the Task Force Talon commandos hurled a grenade at the blazing M-16 fingers.

The Executioner hopped out of the gunship, and bore down on their blind side as the smoky thunderclap cleared the way for the enemy to charge the door.

20

At first, Jabir Nahab didn't trust the moment. The diabolical plot of American soldiers murdering their own and freeing Islamic revolutionaries to lead them to a cache of WMD was so fantastic it defied his imagination. It flew in the face of everything he knew about the enemy. If they could so easily kill their own kind to get what they wanted, surely his number would come up when he was no longer required.

Yes, there was willingness on his part to go along with the mad bloody scheme—what choice did he have?—but there were no altruistic motives on anyone's side of the fence. As for himself, he determined, unless this proved to be a setup to execute any or all of them, he would go along with the plan. Once he was in Turkey, there were contacts, allies among the militant Turks who despised the West. He could link up with them and dish back to this Braden what he had so savagely taken. Once, of course, the WMD was in his possession.

"What are you waiting for? Get your ass in gear!" one of Braden's men shouted.

They hadn't shackled him, and he found that one more interesting tidbit. Were they hoping he lunged for a weapon? He heard the shouting and cursing down the hallway, the din of weapons fire swelling in his cage as moved for the open door. There, he was yanked into the hall by Braden who was shouting orders at his men near the edge of the last cage in line. Something about falling back or fragging them, head for their bird, but the hellish racket of weapons fire, the distant crunch of an explosion was making it near impossible to hear.

And Nahab marveled at the sight of five, maybe six dead Marines strewed down the corridor, the stark white concrete floor running red with infidel blood. He looked at a discarded weapon, hands trembling, eyes wide, then Braden snarled in his ear, "Don't even think about it!"

THE EXECUTIONER HIT the rabble with a 40 mm buckshot round, using one of their hapless lot for his point of impact. As the thug was obliterated in the gory cloud, countless razor-sharp steel bits blew through the cutthroat's heart as the blast. Men were screaming in agony, weapons falling and all but forgotten as they were ravaged by the steel locust swarm. A few simply bled out, toppled as shock took over to finish them off. A few more, howling mad, stood their ground, wheeling toward the source of terrible attack.

Rolling ahead, Bolan saw the two TFT thugs vanish beyond the doorway, and he held down the M-16's trigger. It was a clean sweep of merciless autofire, raking them, left to right and back.

Beyond the litter of bodies, Bolan spied the TFT traitors in the doorway. Pros, not hesitating over the sight of the massacre, they started winging gunfire when Bolan beat them to it, driving them to cover as he sprayed the doorway with a long dousing of 5.56 mm lead. From the sound of it, Braden and thugs were engaged in a firefight with the Marines at some point deep in the core of the facility. With any luck, Bolan thought he might be able to save a few good men. If not, he intended to exact a heavy blood debt from whatever butchers popped up along the way.

He armed a frag grenade and pitched it for the doorway. They came around the corner again, firing, spraying the yard, one of the TFT thugs maybe getting lucky as he spotted the steel egg bouncing up, vanished two heartbeats before the fire cloud blossomed.

The two moaning traitors were treated to a compassion burst they hardly deserved.

Bolan fed his assault rifle a fresh clip and dumped a 40 mm HE round down the M-203's gullet. A check of his compass on the roll, all clear, and the Executioner penetrated the doorway, navigating his course around the bodies on the floor. Homed in on the raging firefight he gauged in progress near the prisoner cages, the Executioner gathered steam to go in search of fresh blood.

"YOUR BUDDY, STONE? He's back and he's presently right up my ass, sir!"

Braden gritted his teeth. Why wasn't he surprised? Hanover was AWOL. There'd been no beefing up the Arab contingent with a few more bodies from a second group. No Poscalar death squad on hand meant the SOB had done a bloody fine number on the whole sorry bunch. Whether planned or coincidentally stumbling into those safehouses— and his money was on the former—before the first shot was even fired, Stone had decimated at least half of the force he was supposed to have storm the compound. The gunship he borrowed certainly aided in getting the bastard back in swift course, under the roof and swinging for the fences if he judged Lieutenant Crawley's sitrep accurately. The big, ballsy one-man wrecking crew, who the hell was he? Who did he really work for? And did it even matter anymore?

"Sir, do you have any answers for me before I get cut to ribbons!?" Crawley's voice came again over the radio.

Under normal circumstances, Braden would have ripped

the young commando's sphincter wide enough to shove a howitzer through for his flip tongue. But Braden had enough problems on an already overflowing plate. In short, Crawley was on his own. If he made the transport, fine. If not, that would simply be one less chunk of cash he'd have to hand out on payday. Assuming there was a pot of gold to dip his hands into at the end of this blood ride.

Keying his com link he snarled at Murphy, Sanders and Andrews to get the prisoners moving. Braden told Crawley, "Keep moving our way, son, but try and hold the bastard back as best you can."

"With what sir? He's holding everything from a harness chocked with frag grenades to a handheld cannon! He fragged Bradley into beef stew and just blew your hired garbage all to hell!"

"Do something, damn it, even if it's wrong!" Braden shouted, fighting back the urge to scream at the kid to take one for the team. He grabbed and shoved the last extremist ahead, the line of orange jumpsuits finally moving out in a sort of shuddering shuffle step. He'd heard enough from Crawley to know hellfire was on the march. If nothing else, Stone had come to play hardball, ready to go the distance, burn them all down. Now that the man knew he had thwarted an ambush, there would be no dialing back the level of anger and determination.

A twenty-foot white shark was headed their way, Braden knew, the scent of blood in his nose.

He was about to order Crawley to link up with his group at the far edge, when the guttural grunt and curse sounded in his ear. The frag blasts began in thunderclapping torque as his men began lobbing one steel baseball after another. The Marines were holding on, cursing and shooting for all they were worth, but Braden wouldn't have expected anything less. The frag show began taking care of that lion pride, clearing his six so he could march east by north, out to their waiting taxi. Unless, of course, Stone came blasting in from behind.

"Crawley?"

He was repeating the soldier's name, suspected the kid had already been devoured by their man-eating problem, when the wall at the far end of the corridor vanished in a cloud of smoke and fire.

ZHABAT SNATCHED THE RPG-7 from al-Habrak. In pairs, his men were trailing Braden's men into the tight confines of the chain-link tunnel, bypassing the corpses of the opening Marine casualties. He knew the assault rifle would prove no match if they ran into an armed force, dug in somewhere and blazing away. There were three more Marine problems at what he assumed was the front door. All of them were winging out autofire, rounds shrieking off the steel housing of the tunnel-cage, the thundering retorts of explosions lighting up the facility behind them. As he crouched, deciding to hang farther back, he saw two of his men grabbing at their chests, slick dark fingers shooting skyward. They were toppling. Zhabat was more afraid than enraged at the sight of his men on their way to Paradise, when a fireball erupted in the doorway. The mangled stick figures were sailing across the no-man's land, Zhabat thinking he could turn around and flee the madness in this sudden burst of mayhem, when Turkle swept over him.

"I want you and your people to storm the front door, move inside! There is a small group of shooters on the way in and they need to be stopped before we can fly on!"

"And where will you go?" Zhabat shouted, as another peal of thunder raked the air.

"That's not your concern, asshole! I'm heading off a threat to the east! Just get your asses inside and help me to outflank them! Go——!"

WHATEVER HELL HAD descended at the deep end of the corridor, Nahab suspected it was not boding well for Braden and his people. In fact, as he looked back, peering into the roiling smoke, he made out the twisted heaps of bodies, a tattered black beret actually fluttering out of the cloud, the wall awash in dribbling blood and gore. Score a fat one, he thought, for the mystery invasion force, or maybe it was a Marine or two, holding on, fighting back against their betrayers.

There was a mauled groaner, maybe two down there, attempting to rise, he saw, bringing guns to bear on the invisible fighting force when two brief but concentrated bursts to their chests pinned them to the wall in a splash of crimson.

Braden and his troops, six in all, were now in their faces, shouting for greater speed, but keeping grim vigilance, just the same, on the unseen source of devastation at the far end. He was about to face front, Braden screaming for them to turn left, when a tall dark figure emerged from the pall and cut loose with autofire. Had it not been for Dbouri, absorbing a round or two in the onslaught, blood and brain matter splattering him in the face, Nahab knew he would have been on his way to Allah.

There was a chance he still might not make it out of there.

His limbs were, however, now well-oiled from a fresh burst of fear and adrenaline. Bulling ahead, he flung himself around the corner, falling into the stampede with his fellow jihadists, Braden and his men going berserk, pounding out return fire from behind.

"Get to the goddamn plane!" he heard Braden roar. "Run!"

WHETHER OR NOT THERE WERE any Marines left standing was moot, as far as beefing up for his own assault. The TFT frag barrage had wiped out another four, maybe five in his wake, though with chewed and amputated limbs scattered here and there, and with thick waves of smoke smothering the carnage, the body count could have climbed another two or three.

The Executioner was on his own.

They were beating a hard flight east by north, which meant they were heading for the transport. Braden and his thugs were winging back the gunfire, the last of the orange jumpsuits vanishing around the edge but not before Bolan tagged one with a lightning jag of 5.56 mm tumblers up the spine. Bolan knew another set of lethal problems, was breaching the facility, sliding, one by one, through the north door. He couldn't be certain, but he suspected they were the Arab militant gang hired on as Braden's butchers.

Bolan sprayed an M-16 burst at the retreating mob, rounds snapping over his head, but not before he managed to bag one more TFT thug, the commando whirling across the corridor, falling, down and apparently forgotten by Braden. Unless he wanted to fall back himself, then cut a long, circuitous route south and attempt to outflank them…

He decided it was not the best idea, considering a new threat had already cropped up on his flank.

A black beret popped into view at the tail end of the pack, the HK 33 stuttering out a long stream that drove Bolan back into the smoke.

His only option was to remove the cannibals heading his way. The Executioner bolted across an adjacent corridor, fell into the cover of an open cage, then lined them up for the grinding touch of a 40 mm greeting.

ZHABAT DECIDED to disobey Turkle and abort the attack. There was no way of telling who or how many were waiting inside the door, he thought, watching as two of his comrades slid through the opening.

They were promptly mowed down by autofire that scythed holes through the drifting smoke, blowing them back out the door, all flailing limbs and jetting blood. The others were howling, in panic or rage it was impossible to say, retracing their ventured steps. A sort of slapstick comedy was underway next, he saw, as arms flapped and tangled together, Jarid and Mohammed slamming, bouncing off each other, scowling and cursing as they stumbled on. Two of his men were pitching to earth, crying out in alarm, when Zhabat glimpsed the blur streaking their way. He knew what was coming. He flung himself to the ground, glimpsed two more figures racing through the doorway when the blast pealed, launching at least one of them overhead, sticky raindrops pattering his face.

He felt the terror turn to nausea, threatening to stake him where he lay, but his fighters left standing reeled into the boiling smoke, hitting firepoints on either side of the jagged maw, unloading assault rifles but at who only knew what. He figured he'd better do something that looked remotely heroic, and fast, or he might lose more than just face. After all, he had called them to arms here, thrust them into the unknown. At the time, it had seemed a wise—or at worst ambitious—decision, but this was more than he chose to tackle. The more he thought about it, the more he suspected they had been duped to play some losing hand in a plot the infidels had concocted to cover their planned escape.

And to go in hunt of the mystery weapon to snap up in their own greedy, murderous hands.

A hard search of the no-man's land fanning east, and Zhabat saw Turkle and a companion moving in an easy stroll that left him wondering just how serious was the threat hitting the facility. Or was it something else entirely?

Looking out to the hangar, noting the ramp on the transport was down, he figured whoever was slated to fly on would soon emerge from inside the prison walls.

Zhabat scraped himself off the ground and hollered for his men to follow.

THE EXECUTIONER HIT the wounded TFT man in the chest with a triburst of 5.56 mm tumblers and moved on. Between the electric charge of combat senses, adrenaline and righteous anger, Bolan was tuned in to the slightest movement or noise, twelve and six. And he didn't need to see them to know they were more than just gallivanting beyond the north wall.

Sensing full retreat, that there was nothing under the prison roof but the dead, the Executioner hit the next corner low, M-16 ready to drop the next shooter.

Clear.

He made the decision on the march, cutting down another bisecting corridor, heading east. Braden, so far, had what he wanted. Having played out his treacherous hand, the load of prisoners was meant to serve his ultimate purpose once they landed in Turkey, the contacts, rendezvous points and such in tow with the extremist passengers. Factor in that Braden had a better idea than he did where the WMD was stashed, and Bolan figured to let him fly, leave the tracking to the Farm.

He had a plan, though, to give Braden a taste of what he could expect in Turkey. And if it brought down the ship, so be it.

His M-16 leading the final turn toward the northern door, the Executioner listened to the night beyond and threw himself against the wall as he saw four armed shadows sweep past. Apparently more than just the TFT brigands were looking to bail Camp Triangle, but if they were looking for a quick and pain-free bon voyage…

Slow and cautious, the Executioner made the opening,

crouched and took in the exodus. They were streaming through the northeast gate at the edge of the motor pool, orange jumpsuits lagging behind Braden and his men. The foursome was picked up the far rear, gaining ground, when two more TFT black berets materialized from the motor pool. They were engaged in an argument that looked poised to turn murderous when Bolan gauged the range, all set to dump yet more grief on the enemy.

This was not a night, the Executioner knew, slipping a finger around the M-203's trigger, for any negotiating.

"JUST WHAT THE HELL do you think you're doing?"

Zhabat was an eye blink away from bringing up the HK 33 and gunning down Turkle and his sidekick when the motor pool, or part of it, vanished before his eyes in fire and smoke. Turkle and the other black beret were sailing from the mushroom cap, close enough to ground zero they appeared to catch and ride a slab of wreckage like some hideous surf board. Zhabat turned away from the rush of searing heat, nosediving and burying his face in the earth, riding out the storm. The sky pelted trash, but Zhabat was on his feet, indifferent to whether the black berets or his own men were alive, thinking he needed to reach the transport before it was airborne, leaving him to perhaps confront Brazilian authorities who would surely come swarming the grounds.

The only refuge lay in the waiting arms of his brothers in jihad. Hadn't he attempted to do what Turkle wanted? And whoever was really in charge would already be boarding the transport, he believed, never knowing he hadn't fired a single shot in anger. And if it was intelligence the infidels wanted on the WMD in Turkey he had a few facts squirreled away in his head he could present as a bargaining chip.

He needed salvation from this hell first.

Zhabat spotted the first batch hitting the ramp, several of

his imprisoned comrades stumbling onto the runway. As he surged out of the gate, both amazed and annoyed to find his surviving brothers on his heels, Zhabat began thinking they weren't falling from exhaustion out there.

And yet another horror slowly dawned on him that they were being sniped from some point behind. Looking back, he saw his brothers pointing, followed their flapping arms and bugged out eyes to the source of their fear. He was searching the stretch of ground, dreading, praying to Allah an invisible bullet did not drop him, then made out the tall shadow just as Mohammed cried out and slammed to the earth. He clutched his leg, a thick jet of dark crimson spurting between his fingers, screaming for someone to help. Bless al-Habrak, he thought, as his cousin began to haul the wounded man to his feet, sparing him the task of having to explain himself later for having abandoned him to bleed to death. That, of course, assumed any of them even made the plane.

Zhabat next found himself transfixed by the sight, the incredible thought dancing through his mind whether or not one lone gunman could have possibly been responsible for the death and destruction he'd witnessed up to then. His imagination was inflamed with visions of scores of bodies strewed all over the facility. One gunman was chasing all of them to the plane?

He urged greater speed from his legs, saw then heard two, maybe three of his cousins in orange jumpsuits calling for help, sprawled on the turf, clutching bloodied limbs. For whatever reason, the transport plane was gaining speed, the scream locked in his throat, the ramp kicking up a trail of sparks as the mammoth bird began rumbling down the runway.

Suddenly, lungs heaving, fearing his heart would explode out his chest from exertion, he found it strange no more bodies were dropping at the grim touch of the lone gunman. The temptation to look back overpowering him. It was only a whirling glance, from the shadow with the massive rocket launcher in hand to the tanker trucks and fuel bins, before the first explosion set the world on fire.

As the tidal wave of flames reached out, Zhabat screamed and braced himself to be incinerated.

THE BELLOW OF PURE RAGE sounded a minuscule bleating in his ears, all but squashed by the roaring of the conflagration. Wincing, Braden was forced to turn away for a moment as the blinding mountain of fire kept on growing, surging outward. Glancing back, it was gathering what he could only imagine was supernova might with each tanker and bin that blew in turn, all thunder and white brilliance. He had no clue how much fuel was being ignited to eat up everything in the onrushing billows. He slammed a fist into the wall panel, saw the ramp shudder up the first foot or so, but feared he was too late.

The shock waves rolled over the fuselage next. Braden tumbled into the wall against the vicious invisible jolt. The terrorists were crying out behind him, a wail of the damned, to be sure, hitting the deck, with his troops holding on but throwing their faces away as superheated wind rushed in, a belch from the bowels of hell.

He hit the intercom, as thunderbolts drummed over the roof, yet more meteors pounding the walls. Braden feared shock waves alone would lift the bird off its wheels, flip them, end over end, in flying acrobatics of smashed skulls and broken bones. "More speed, damn it! Get us up and out of here before we're all charred meat!" he screamed at the pilot.

Braden heard the shrieking of men being burned alive. He shuffled to the opening, found himself both enthralled and horrified by the dam burst of fire, as dragon spray funnels ap-

peared to fuse and sweep over those hapless few who sur-
vived the blasts. Flaming human comets went thrashing
across the runway, flailing on the ground in vain attempts to
extinguish devouring shrouds of fire. Braden squinting as the
fire wind gusted in his face. It occurred to him that if Stone
had wanted to blow the bird off the runway he would have
done so. And he gathered a good suspicion why the SOB had
chosen to let them fly on.

The ramp was closing, not fast enough for his liking, but
Braden spotted a lone figure clear the mushroom heads, hurling his assault rifle away as he pumped his arms and legs and
lunged for the ramp. One guy, he thought, had managed to
save his bacon from getting fried. Reaching down and fisting a hand full of hair, Braden hauled him through the space
with a foot to spare and shouted in the face of terror, "And
just who might you be?"

CHOICES.

Every bend in the road of life had them, and Bolan was
never of the mind to question one once it was made. Running the table by blasting the transport to scrap would have
been a fitting coup de grâce under different choices, but
Braden had just become his own hunk of chum.

Bigger man-eaters were on the loose somewhere.

Sometimes, the enemy stole another day or so by default
and circumstance.

It happened.

It was raining pure hell on the runway, and the Executioner
spared a mercy burst each from his M-16 for two devils. He
felt the scorching heat, mindful of how quickly he had fallen
back when the first tanker of super high-test fuel was touched
off. Two more sixty-ones, an HE and incendiary missile kept
the vision of hell on earth marching.

Bolan took in the utter devastation. The hangar was reduced to smoking hills of rubble. All birds vaporized to molten scrap or blown halfway back to Ciudad del Este. Dozens of yards of east fencing had been blown down or irradiated to flowing silver creeks by the fiery tornados. The sky was still crashing around the armory and motor pool, the larger slabs pounding through the roofs of two Humvees, when Bolan spied a mad dog in black beret shuddering to his feet, HK subgun up and swinging his way.

The Executioner hit Turkle full in the chest with a 3-round send-off.

Bolan gave the runway a thorough search, as the transport lifted off, barely clearing the fence line.

Gone, in search of their hallowed WMD.

He didn't give the bird another look as he dialed up Michaels on his com link. Littered for a good hundred yards west with wreckage, if the runway couldn't accommodate the Gulfstream, which was in a holding pattern to the east, then Bolan would have his men find a suitable stretch of grassland.

As he told Michaels to pick him up, the Executioner gave the hell of Camp Triangle a last look. What had happened here, he suspected, was simply a prelude to something far darker and more insidious.

So be it.

Bolan knew the final outcome, the sum total of any war was only as good as the next battle. Braden was in the wind, but the Executioner determined his number on the wheel of misfortune was coming up.

The enemy could expect final rough justice when he tracked them down and snatched away the dreams of savages.

Nothing more, nothing less.

21

The truth was gaining on Murat Ghirgulz the hard way. As he searched the Turk military unit through the Russian field glasses, attempting to get a fix on enemy numbers, he began to believe he was finally getting somewhere in his quest. That the Turk wild dogs were presently combing through the smoking rubble of their latest campaign of genocide against his people in what they called the province of Agri told Ghirgulz they were getting close. The only question remaining to be answered was which side would get to the cache first.

For what felt like endless months now, he and his clan of fighters, aligned albeit loosely with the Kurdistan Workers Party, had been both hunters and hunted as they wandered the mountainous nowhere along the Iranian border. They forged north as the carnage mounted on both sides, the hit-and-run guerrilla warfare pushing them deep into the frontier near the Russian border, as the information leaked to him from tongues screaming in agony.

So much death, so much blood on his hands. If he thought about it, there was truly nothing left but pain, suffering, and death, though he intended to be on the giving end until he drew his last breath in the struggle for Kurdish autonomy.

Nothing left but to keep going. Keep fighting. Keep killing.

Like many of his cousins, squeezed beside him in the

boulder-studded pocket, Ghirgulz had no family, no village in Kurdistan to return to, if and when the battles ever ended. The Turks had recently launched new attacks against villages, from Hakkari near the Iraqi border to roughly their present position a day's walk northeast of Dogubeyazit. They had one downed Black Hawk gunship to their credit, some Turk blood along with a few Kurd informants on their hands as the result of torture, but not even a million enemy dead would ease in his mind the pain of losing his wife and four children to the Turk butchers. With each enemy body, though, Ghirgulz learned what the Turks and their Iraqi bootlickers were after, why they were killing people in one of the most vicious and bloody campaigns he could ever recall.

Ghirgulz looked up. They were in the foothills on the south face of Agri Dagi. He guessed their altitude at somewhere around six or seven hundred feet. Even at this relatively low height the icy air was difficult to breathe, forcing them to cover their mouths and noses with bandannas cut from wool, lest running mucus freeze in their nostrils. How high they needed to climb he couldn't say, but figured the Turks or their Iraqi minions knew. The morning mist would thicken, the snow would deepen as they climbed the treacherous face. The summit, he believed, was some five thousand feet plus, but without oxygen and more to cover them than wool trousers and coats, he couldn't imagine they could ascend much higher than two thousand feet.

He had heard the tales over the years from men who had allegedly climbed near to the top, accidentally stumbling across the splintered ruins of what they claimed was a giant, ancient boat, wedged frozen into the surface of a glacier. Myth or truth, he didn't much care, but a part of him tended to believe this land—that had seen so much bloodshed since the time of the ancients of Anatolia—could, indeed, feel the wrath of a God who would bury the world in flood, though spare a chosen few to repopulate a new Earth, man and animal alike. That in mind, he savored the image of himself, an avenging arm of the Almighty, slaying the Turk hordes, Kurdistan rising from the ashes of the war he would soon declare.

And the instrument of his vengeance was somewhere in these mountains. If—no, when—he seized the cache he would unleash death of epic proportion that would rival the story of the Great Flood.

He watched, as the soldiers he knew responsible for burning their village, raping their women and murdering anything that walked or crawled, fanned out and the armored personnel carriers, Humvees and transports rolled into a smoke-and-corpse free zone. They fell out of canvas-covered transports, quickly began unfurling and erecting tents. Satellite dishes were uncrated, generators hauled from truck beds as they constructed a hasty makeshift camp. They were staying, but for how long?

Scanning the carnage, he watched as a Turk soldier toed a body. Ghirgulz thought he saw the body move, then the soldier drilled a short burst into the chest.

He had seen enough, as he caught the echo another burst of autofire ringing up from the valley. Rising, AK-47 in hand, he ordered his snipers with the scoped Dragunov rifles to take up positions along a ledge he indicated some thirty feet higher. Then he climbed a tortuous path along a precipice, careful not to kick loose a stone before his boots sank into a half-foot of snow.

The smell of roasting flesh and loosened bowels guided him into the cave. Six of his top lieutenants, he found, were standing near the fire, but they appeared more interested in the grisly sack of raw meat staked to the ground than keeping warm. Closing, he found the informant had been fileted around the chest and ribs some more since he'd left them to their grim task of extracting information. The stench of fresh urine told him they had attempted to revive Apo Buccalah, but he had seen enough men skinned alive to know when they were past the point of no return. Still, the Kurd traitor was clinging to life, Ghirgulz making out the faint gagging noises, muffled by the wool rag. He looked at Birdal, who shook his head, and told him, "I am afraid we will get nothing more out of this jackal."

For the moment, Ghirgulz decided they had enough to at least stand by and watch what happened in the valley. Without hesitation, he lifted his assault rifle and pumped a quick burst into the traitor's chest.

THE BLACK HAWK CLAIMED a landing zone near the fuel bin. As he marched from his command post, little more than a stone hovel, and vectored for the large tent where they were gathered for the daily briefing on operations in the northern Iraqi frontier, Major Alan Hawke hated himself. But he knew there was no choice.

Not if he wished to continue breathing.

Although what he was prepared to do was the ultimate crime against God, country and humanity, he reasoned the ends justified the means in his case.

They had to.

He had sold his soul long ago, he knew, but it had nothing to do with money or power, though the former would certainly assist him in vanishing to points unknown. In about two days, maybe less, the United States of America as he knew it would cease to exist. Either he was on board or he would be fed to the sharks. He had taken their money to keep silent, or inform them about what they suspected may be left in the region by way of WMD. He'd been ordered by them—without the knowledge of CENTCOM—to search out and eliminate any Iraqis linked to the pre-war smuggling operation. As for his personal life, he supposed it eased the pain of the coming task, was a salve for his conscience to know there was nothing left for him in terms of family back in the States. There would be no golden years with a loved one by his side, no grandchildren at his feet. Nothing left but to put it all—which, in reality, was nothing—behind, march into the future.

Hawke checked his watch. High noon. Right on schedule. He watched the tall figure in black fatigues, black beret with the Task Force Talon emblem and wielding an HK 33 hop from the helicopter, he wanted to tell himself that the revolutionary change about to ignite a firestorm of anarchy in America was for the eventual salvation of the country. Up to a point, he believed in their rebellion, having seen too many changes himself in a country he'd once loved and fought for to sit idly on the sidelines and watch the savages tear down democracy and rebuild it in their own wicked, selfish image, where greed and immorality were the gods they worshiped. The question begged itself as to how much better off America would be when it fell under the iron fist of military rule. Perhaps democracy—given the one constant that was human nature, with all its faults, flaws and follies—was simply a failed experiment, he decided, but one that required a different hands-on approach, or rather a fine tuning in order to rejuvenate what good was once there.

As the Black Hawk's flight crew hit the ground running to refuel for the return trip, Hawke looked at the face of the man he thought of as Death incarnate, the assassin already plucking a frag grenade off his webbing. He went by many names, one of those black ops who would never show up on any intelligence agency's radar screens, and the killer he knew as Locklin was there to make sure he fulfilled his role.

He took one last sweeping look at the broken tableland. There was nothing out there in the rock and scrub wasteland save for a roving band of Bedouin. Hawke raised his M-16.

He hung back at the flap, as Locklin vanished down the other side. A moment later he heard the thunderclap, the blast signaling him to enter the future. For a fleeting second, he balked at those shouts of anger, cries of pain, then charged through the flap and began doing his grim part, telling himself these young soldiers were dying for a better America.

22

Logistics alone would prove a monumental task. After he laid out his suspicions to Hal Brognola over the sat link about the danger he felt the President was in under his own roof, the big Fed, he knew, had been scrambling. To cover everything Bolan needed, Brognola was juggling back-channeled calls from his Justice Department office to key contacts in the military and intelligence communities. The Farm was doing its part to park a satellite over the area to gather whatever intelligence he needed for the next phase.

Brognola and the Stony Man team had never let him down when it came to ironing out the finer details of hardware, contacts, insertion, and Bolan knew they wouldn't pull any punches now. Just the same, he felt his nerves taut as piano wire. The knockout blow was up to him but still a way off in the wings, as he worked on a cup of coffee in the Gulfstream's workstation.

At this juncture, given what he knew and suspected, patience was best left to the angels. Perusing satellite imagery and computer-printed flight charts, it was easily a nine-thousand-mile flight by the route they were taking to Incirlik American Air Base in Adana along the Mediterranean Sea. At top cruising speed of 521 mph, the Gulfstream's range was good for forty-two hundred miles. That meant two refueling stops. Brognola struck gold on that score. Bolan's original

Bogotá fuel stop before hitting the Triangle on the way in was switched to Caracas, Venezuela where the big Fed unearthed a CIA contact with in-country pull. That put them a few hundred miles closer to Madrid, and even then Bolan knew they'd damn near be redlining their way in at the end of the transatlantic flight.

Already the morning was grinding on, and they had just hit Venezuelan airspace, needing to cover ten time zones from there before landing at Incirlik. And how much of a head start did Braden have? The Executioner believed the Task Force Talon leader had his own travel arrangements worked out in advance. He was thinking the transport bird— even customized for auxiliary tanks, slimmed down from the C-130 version, built for speed and distance—would cut the path of shortest and least resistance on a straight northeast vector, maybe having greased officials in one of the West African countries.

He drew a deep breath, let it out slowly, aware his mind was racing. It was going to be a long flight, twenty to twenty-four hours or more, depending on time lost on the ground for fuel stops, no matter how efficiently Brognola kept the wheels spinning.

There was no point, Bolan knew, rehashing the treachery in the Triangle, the subsequent slaughter. The wreckage—legal, political or otherwise—was best left for others to clean up, sort out. He was a soldier, and his job was to keep on kicking ass.

As earlier agreed, the President would be kept in the dark about Camp Triangle for as long as possible while Brognola shipped in his own team of Justice and FBI agents to secure what was essentially a sprawling graveyard. He was bypassing all normal channels in that regard, protocol tossed out the window as he risked career or worse, but he understood Bolan's line of reasoning. If this Special Countermeasure Task

Force was plotting some kind of palace coup, Bolan didn't want them on full alert, though he had to reckon Braden would sound the SOS. There was no point, he knew, getting swept up in myriad hypotheticals and worst-case scenarios.

"You understand what you're asking, Striker, is unprecedented."

"It's an unprecedented situation, Hal."

"Forget the idea that you have the Man authorize me in the event…and before an event we don't even know will transpire."

"I'm only looking for some trust on the Man's part."

"Oh, it would be a definite show of trust, I'll grant you that. I just don't know how much longer I can hold off running your scenario from A to Z by the Man. With all you're asking him to give you, he's going to want specifics, as in facts before he hands you the keys to the White House and the other free pass you mentioned. If it goes down the way you suspect, you understand we're not the only game in town, covert or otherwise."

"Understood. I know I'm stating the obvious, Hal, but each administration has used us specifically because we are at the top of their list for deniable expendables. He's still a politician, he reads the polls, and if this thing is headed where I think, it might his approval rating won't mean squat if this whole mess sees him staring at impeachment, assuming he's still breathing."

There was a long pause on Brognola's end of the line before he said, "All right. In light of that argument, I think I might be able to persuade him to see it your way, without going into too much detail. Say he keeps the snakes right in front of him from here on, it makes sense, at least we know where they are. And if he can't, I'll dispatch my own team to monitor their movements around town. Okay, I'll light a fire, you'll get what you want."

Bolan could believe that. He knew from long experience the clout the big Fed wielded when it came to national security. Successful track records had a way of speaking for themselves, even converting those skeptics bent on straddling the fence, finger in the air to see which way the wind blew.

The Executioner listened as Brognola informed him he had the carte blanche of a Presidential Directive when he hit Incirlik. It was already in the hands of a Major General Eugene Thomas of Special Forces who reported directly to CENTCOM. It was nonnegotiable where the Man stood, since Brognola had at least made him aware of the ongoing hunt for the WMD. Colonel Brandon Stone was part of the team, or he was out, though he would share command. Bolan agreed, but would call his own action on the spot, depending on which way that covert wind blew, adding the possibility he might need a fast ride back to the States.

"Consider it done. By the way, your prisoner's story so far checks out."

Bolan looked at the back of Mohammed Bal-Ada's head as Brognola ran down the investigation particulars he'd dug up through the CIA, NSA and Interpol, but added he couldn't be one-hundred-percent positive the Syrian was clean.

"In other words, whatever your gut tells you about him, it's your call," Brognola said. "But I don't see the CIA chauffeuring him back home to Syria."

"I'm cutting him loose at Incirlik, unless, that is, a red flag is raised on your end."

"I'm sure you already know this, but the spooks will want to talk to him some more before they ring him up a taxi."

"Understood," Bolan said, perusing the satellite imagery of his destination. He could use Bal-Ada's knowledge and experience in the region to point out the exact area where he'd encountered the Turks and Iraqis.

"Striker, I get the feeling there's something you want to tell me."

Bolan took a deep breath. How well his old friend knew him, he thought. "It was just a thought, a touch of paranoia maybe, and with no proof…for now, I'd just as soon keep it to myself, Hal."

"But you're thinking I can add two-and-two on why you want me tell the President as little as possible, unless absolutely boxed into a corner by the Man." Brognola sighed.

Bolan picturing the big Fed sitting at his desk, a knotted bellyful of coffee and antacid tablets, gnawing on one cigar after the other. He probably hadn't slept since before the mission began.

"Let's hope to God you're wrong," Brognola said, and the line went dead.

Bolan gathered up the pile of satellite imagery. He would have a chat with Bal-Ada, and, if possible, a combat nap, though he doubted any rest would come. He was sore, bruised and busted, weary to the bone. But he was alive, and he was hungry to get to the next hellzone and burn down the enemy.

Rising, his thoughts echoed the big Fed's ominous sentiments. He hoped he was dead wrong. If the President of the United States was using the Special Countermeasure Task Force as an instrument of revolution…

For the time being he chalked it up to the ghosts of the conspiracy burned down in his wake. If the President gave him all he asked for, went the extra mile on the trust score, then the matter was settled. If not…

Bolan shut down the mental picture before it took full dark shape. Why buy phantom trouble, when there was plenty of real trouble to be had.

23

"I have a bad feeling it's all set to fall apart."

Lee Durham steepled his fingers, looking around the tight quarters of his West Wing office, crunching numbers while grunting at Ralph Griswald. Space—if he could call it that—in the sixty-by-ninety-foot West Wing was virtually nonexistent, his own cubicle, he figured, roughly seventy square feet. The Oval Office, a few long strides down from his door, measured thirty-six-feet long by thirty wide. Considering those dimensions, he knew what would be removed from inside the Kevlar vests his security force wore at all times would be more than sufficient. A little here in his office, the bulk of it spread around in the Oval Office when the time came, would get the job done. The basement was another matter, figure a hundred-plus personnel, down below, in what was essentially a minicorporation of kitchen staff and other service flunkies. With luck, the ceiling would drop on their heads. But it was the West Wing, where the real moving and shaking took place, that held the keys to his kingdom. If he was forced to—and he didn't think the President would let it get that far—everything from the Oval Office and the adjoining President's study, clear down to the National Security Adviser's office, the Cabinet Room and on up through the second floor…

And then there would be what he secretly coined Big

Mama. He pictured the moment of triumph when he dropped that bomb—or the threat of using it. Who would beg him not to do it? Would the President, or the chief of staff or whoever else happened to be there perhaps even kneel before him, groveling, kissing ass to save their world, spouting righteous indignation? Curse him as traitor? Spare the masses, the voting public, for God's sake, something like that? Or would they stand tall, forget the politics and the polls, show some guts? Would the chief executive crumble, grant him coronation on the spot? Or would he be forced to execute a top aide, maybe shoot the National Security Adviser or the Chairman of the Joint Chiefs, splash their brains all over the President's Resolute Table to get them in gear to meet his nonnegotiable demands?

Soon, and, oh, how glorious it would all be.

He looked at Griswald, sitting there in the wingback chair in front of his desk, gnawing on his lip, nerves on fire now that the hour of truth was nearly upon them. The man was beginning to annoy him.

"I read the President's mood at our daily brief, and I can't say I'm encouraged," Griswald said. Durham thought the man had sprouted a few more gray hairs the past several hours, the sagging jowl drooping low enough it seemed to perch on his open necktie. "Suddenly, he's postponed his socalled Mideast Peace Sojourn and his meeting in Pakistan with their president."

"And?"

"Well, not to mention it was us who busted our tails putting together the whole logistical package, the security, but the sudden manner in which he appears to dismiss our effort, his ear now more tuned and attentive to his chief of staff, the Joint Chiefs, the National Security Adviser, when up to now they all fairly seethed with envy because it was our word and our work he showed favor—"

Durham waved a hand, frowning. "If it's praise and recognition you want then you chose the wrong career, Mr. Griswald."

"How can you be so glib?"

"Not glib—confident."

"How? With what we know happened last night down there, your man on the way with a load of fundamentalists…"

Durham swept his office daily for bugs, but he'd been a spook too long to trust that the walls didn't have ears. "Careful," he said.

"Doesn't it concern you that the President has made no mention of what clearly is not just a disaster but what could prove to become an international scandal? With potential impeachment implications? A fiasco, of which he will want an explanation from us. A thorough investigation is sure to follow, one that could see our scalps hung from his desk, since everyone in this town is always looking for a scapegoat. Those were our people, recommended, recruited by us."

In fact, it did trouble him, but he wasn't about to let Griswald know that. "Again, please choose your words with more caution," Durham said in warning.

Griswald snorted. "If they knew, I figure we'd be staring down the whole of the Secret Service by now."

Durham heaved a breath. The man needed to gird his loins, show some courage. Yes, there were problems to solve, but only in the short term. The Braden situation, for one, was baffling all by its lonesome, what with some one-man firestorm none of them could get any intelligence on razing the Camp Triangle compound. Word was sure to reach the President any moment. Or was there some other demon, lurking in the shadows behind the scenes? Was the President jealously guarding his own knowledge of the disaster in Brazil? Waiting to spring it on them? If forced to confront the situation, he would hand Braden's head to the President. His file on the man sat on his desk, ready to deliver. He would come clean about the missing WMD, a stall tactic, to be sure, until the special delivery was made to his room at the Embassy Suites.

"I almost envy Rubin," Griswald muttered into his tie.

"What was that?"

"Rubin. I said—"

"I heard you, I just wanted you to say it in a voice becoming of a man and not a mouse. Hear me but good, Griswald. His task is of no small importance," Durham growled. "As for what you wish, keep in mind that he is prepared to sacrifice his life. Are you?"

Griswald scowled, eyes flaring.

Good, Durham thought, anger was good.

"If I weren't, I would have walked a long time ago."

That's better, Durham thought, proud of himself to be pushing all the right buttons, and said, "Then it's settled."

"What is?"

"Your cold feet. Don't bring them to the big show."

"What about security?"

Durham chuckled. "We are security. I don't care how you think you read the President's dark mood. Understand something, my friend. The President created us. We are already, for the most part, albeit secretly, the administration. He doesn't want the public, the press, not even those assholes in the Senate and Congress to be aware we exist. We're just rising to the next highest level."

"And when, precisely, is our ascent to the next level going to happen?"

"That I can't be positive of. The special delivery is en route, that's all I can say. I cannot make our courier move any faster without a lapse in both judgment and security."

"Say our hand is forced—"

"Then I am prepared to act on the spot."

Durham saw Griswald was ready to pursue more anxieties, when the phone rang. He was grateful for the interruption, blood pressure pulsing in his ears, and nearly snatched up the receiver. It was the chief of staff. The President wanted to see them in the Oval Office right away. The ass-kissing toad was pissing in his ear, implying SCTF had better damn well have something for the President on who was behind the executions in Jordan, like they swore they'd have by the end of day's business.

"Who was that?" Griswald asked as Durham slammed down the receiver.

Durham smiled, suddenly enjoyed watching his partner-in-treason squirm. "The chief of staff."

"And?"

Durham leaned back in his chair, smile holding as he envisioned one moment of the coming glory. "And, I was just thinking…"

"What?"

"That the self-righteous brown-nosed prick might be the first one I shoot."

24

General Osman Ataturk sometimes had to inform the paltry few historically knowledgeable foreigners he was no relation to the hero of the War of Independence and founder of modern secular Turkish democracy. Much like the CIA assassin named Locklin and the Special Forces Major Hawke standing before him in his tent, the culturally aware often seemed disappointed when he informed as much, as if no blood link made him less of a leader of fighting men.

They could kindly kiss his hairy Turk ass, he thought.

In the case of ignorant foreigners who didn't know or care about the truth—Kurd garbage looking to undermine the State through terrorism—whatever they thought they believed of him was furthest from the truth. He was no political stooge. He was no intermediary bagman, out here to glad-hand for office. His hands had personally shed so much blood in the Kurd-controlled southeast area of Turkey, he was known as Ataturk the Terrible. The American intelligence operatives, he was fairly certain, knew who he really was.

If they did, the Americans didn't appear impressed by his fearsome reputation.

Almost a day and a half since setting up camp at the base of the southern foothills of Mount Ararat, and he was forced to wait on Colonel Braden and his militant pack of prisoners, one of whom, allegedly, knew precisely where the

WMD was stockpiled in the mountains. Naturally, he had his own contacts, informants, between Kurd, Iraqi and former intelligence operatives of the Turkish MIT. Some of them were no longer among the living, once their tongues flapped enough about the truth of the WMD. Some were still on the loose, gathering intelligence, swearing to report back, but mostly in hopes of clipping a few more dollars from his numbered Kuwaiti account, as they were on his payroll. The WMD, he believed, had been choppered at some point roughly two thousand feet up the southern slopes. His inside man was reluctant to give him the exact location, details on the number and type of shells, but he was presently watching the store. In truth, it had been the Huey gunship loaner from one of his many airfields that had assisted in delivering the cargo for the Iraqi criminals. The problem on his informant's end—or so stated during near two months' delay— was money, since, his source informed him, the Iraqis were haggling over price, waiting on their contacts inside Turkey to show up with duffel bags full of cash.

The bartering was about to end.

Feeling the scowl again twisting his face, Ataturk looked at his American counterparts. He had been watching Locklin and Hawke consume his tea and smoke his cigarettes for hours on end, poring over both CIA and Turkish MIT satellite imagery and aerial recon photos of the foothills, slopes, gorges and glaciers. Thick cloud cover hindered clear and accurate surveillance photos, making Ataturk wonder just what the two Americans could be searching for. Weather, of course, was a major concern, as far as a quick chopper ride up the side of the mountain. There was wind shear. There was freezing cold. There was heavy cloud cover, which would render visibility next to zero. They grumbled each time he mentioned these problems. They sniffed the air, blew smoke his way. They glanced at him with thinly veiled contempt while helping themselves to another cup of tea or cigarette.

They, of course, had all the answers.

The trouble was, he needed them to get that WMD, but the waiting was fraying his last nerve, while stirring a bubbling caldron of anger in his belly. Against his better judgment, he was in constant contact with one of his Black Hawk crews, having ordered them to recon the gorge he believed led the way to where the Iraqis and their Turk allies—one of whom was his eyes and ears—were sitting on the WMD. Visibility was decent, up to fifteen hundred feet, then the cloud cover became so thick a man could walk on it, or so his crew informed him.

As the Americans muttered to themselves, Ataturk fielded another call from his Black Hawk crew. He heard how they had spotted the Kurds he had been hunting for months—with little more to show for his effort than a few bloody skirmishes—before they vanished into the mountains like ghosts. Presently, they were climbing up the mountain, clearing the thousand-foot line, reaching higher.

They knew something he did not.

Ataturk handed the receiver to his radioman and turned to the Americans. "Gentlemen, I have confirmation of Kurd rebels in the area."

"Yeah?" Locklin said. "So?"

He walked up to the maps and imagery spread over the large metal table and stabbed the area above the southern gorge leading in. "They are moving. Here."

"Again, so what?" Locklin was sneering.

"They, I believe, are after the same ordnance we are, if my source is correct. I have been hunting for them for some time, but these mountain Turks have proved elusive. They killed some of my soldiers. Vengeance, as you might know, is a time-honored tradition in Turkey."

"Okay, and?"

Ataturk kept his anger in check. "I believe it wise to go ahead and begin our own search at this time without further delay. But understand, I intend to engage these rebels along the way."

Locklin checked his watch. "Our man has landed in-country, General. They've already transferred to a Black Hawk. We go when he gets here with our Iraqi guide, and not a minute before. And, understand this—you grease some salve on your Kurd hemorrhoid on your own time."

"I do not expect they will let that happen, as you so eloquently put it. Also, I have been informed by my source at Incirlik that a large American special ops force is en route, likewise believed to be going after the ordnance."

He saw that finally got their attention, their smug looks turning dark with anger, as Hawke growled, "And you chose to only tell us this now, why?"

He was about to tell them it was because they were too busy taking advantage of his hospitality and good nature when Locklin grabbed his radio as it crackled with an unfamiliar voice.

"They're here," the CIA assassin announced, grabbing up his HK 33.

Ataturk wheeled and followed the Americans outside. He watched as the Black Hawk dropped down, settled in its rotor wash by his own gunships, one of which included an Apache he intended to take into battle. The Americans could squawk all they wanted, but every Kurd clan he wiped out was one less murdering band of criminal and terrorist rabble to worry about in the future. Shrugging the heavy wool topcoat higher up on to his shoulders, he clapped his hands at a soldier, who tossed him one of the new American M-16/M-203 combos, feeling a flush of pride as he smoothly caught the assault rifle.

Battle time.

Despite the reluctance or indifference of the Americans, Ataturk intended to blow the Kurds off the face of the mountain. One well-placed Hellfire missile should do it. If he didn't, he knew they would draw first blood, but the arrogant Americans didn't seem to understand that. Yes, he knew, it was Locklin who had first approached him long ago with the offer to find, seize and divide the WMD among themselves. Yes, the assassin was a walking directory of invaluable and critical military and intelligence contacts in his country, and had apparently ingratiated himself to key politicians and intelligence operatives with his knowledge of ongoing terrorist operations in Turkey. But he wasn't any more important, Ataturk decided, beyond getting him what was up the mountain. As often happened when there was a shooting war, friendlies had a way of getting caught in the line of fire. He had been considering how to get rid of the Americans once they helped him capture the WMD, but now there were more special ops on the way.

A conspiracy within a riddle enclosed by an adder's nest was at work, he thought. The mountain was about to become overcrowded. He only hoped it was littered with the right bodies. It was his country, his province, after all, and that WMD should rightfully fall into his hands.

Head bent, Ataturk trailed Locklin and Hawke into the rotor wash. It was easy enough to see who were commandos of Task Force Talon. They wore black hoods, matching berets with their screaming hawk insignia, carried HK submachine guns, Beretta side arms and had webbing heavy with spare clips and grenades. He counted five black hoods crammed near the doorway, then one of the commandos bounded out of the fuselage, a man in an orange jumpsuit in tow.

"Mr. Locklin and Major Hawke."

"Good of you to make the party, Colonel Braden," Locklin said. "Things are heating up and the good general here wants to get moving."

"I concur. We're losing daylight."

"And we may have company up our six."

"Do tell."

"When we're in the air."

Ataturk was beginning to feel like a third wheel, as Braden flashed the whites of his eyes in a look he read as still more contempt.

"This is Nahab," Braden told them. "Claims he's personally been to the stash site."

"It is no claim," the prisoner, said, shivering in his jumpsuit, stamping his feet.

"We'll see," Locklin said. "You ride with us."

"And my deal?" Nahab asked.

Ataturk started, wondering what Braden had promised the terrorist. "What deal?" he questioned.

"Get your convoy moving into the gorge, General," Locklin snapped. "I want that Apache out front of us the whole way in and up! And that crew follows my every order!"

"What deal?" he barked at Braden.

"Goddammit, we don't have time for this crap!" Locklin shouted as he led Nahab away by the arm, marching toward his Black Hawk, the rotors spinning, hurling more grit and dust over Ataturk.

Cursing, Ataturk spun on his soldiers, barking for the convoy and his gunships to move out. The Americans, he suspected, were playing games, looking to cut him out of the load. And now, with what he suspected was an American or joint Special Forces ops of perhaps his own countrymen on the way…

What did the Americans say? he thought. First come, first served, that was it.

Or in this case, first blood first served.

"THEY'RE COMING! Go, go, go!"

Faisal Mohammed, snapping up his AK-47, kept scream-ing at his men for greater speed. He found several of his fight-ers appearing none to eager to move away from the warmth of the fire barrels. He stood his ground in the great bowl-shaped depression, letting his eyes fill with what he had up to then considered a stroke of genius.

Was this a moment of coming triumph, or doom?

It had taken endless and arduous months to transport the cargo safely across the borders of Syria, Iran and his own country of birth. Well in advance of when the infidels began bombing Baghdad—and even into the months of occupation by the Great Satan—the top-ranking intelligence officer in charge of weapons production had personally been granted the honor by the former President to smuggle the cargo out of Iraq. He'd been blessed with suitcases stuffed with Amer-ican currency in hundred-dollar bills to pave the way into Turkey, buy the necessary contacts, assure safe haven. He tended to believe it was more luck, guile and preying on the greed of the Turks. That they had transferred, however, nearly all of what wasn't buried in the deserts outside Baghdad and arrived safely meant Allah had great plans of glory and ret-ribution in store for the Iraqi people.

He stared at the future, determined to save it.

Finding the cave, massive and deep, had been something of a miracle all by itself. It was bitterly cold this high up, but the depth and width of the cave provided them with room to spare to house the cargo. By truck, by mule and horse, what-ever it took, and then the Huey gunship had finally delivered the cargo here. The helicopter was parked on the glacier and covered by black tarp. Each piece, every crate had been moved in here by hand. Hundreds of shells, he observed, ran-ging in various sizes, stood, held together by thick wire. There were crates, piled three and four high, storing the smaller artillery shells and warheads that were custom-made to be fitted to a rocket launcher. There were missiles with stabilizing fins that could be mounted on gunship rocket pods. There were surface-to-surface missiles with a range of up to five hundred kilometers. And then there were the canisters, the next step up, he knew, to martyrdom by jihad bombing. He watched, torn between pride and fear, as three of his men wrapped the vests around their torsos, the canisters already wired, primed to blow with the touch of a button.

They knew what to do when the enemy landed on the glacier.

They had smuggled a little over five thousand pieces. Most of it was VX nerve gas, but there was a smattering of anthrax, botulin, small pox. Enough, he knew, to spread the fear through the infidel occupation force, drive them from his country. The question now remained, would he get the chance?

He looked at his radioman who was in constant contact with their spotter, hidden below on a precipice near the top of the gorge. "How many?" he demanded.

Khalik looked aghast, as he answered, "A convoy is now entering the gorge. Eleven vehicles, most of them troop transports. Three Black Hawks and one Apache."

Battalion strength, then, he assumed, as Khalik guessed at the number of soldiers.

And there were the Kurds, he knew, nearly thirty-strong, scaling whatever tortuous pathways they could find leading up from the gorge.

War was coming to the mountain.

That the Turk military had not made a move before now surprised him, but he had his suspicions why they held back, waiting until this time to make their encroachment. He watched, as Colonel Mahmudah Dagul and his four-man contingent of former Turk intelligence officers descended the short sloping path into the bowl.

"If you intend a suicide stand, after all the sweat and anxiety I went through to secure you and the cargo here, I urge you allow me to attempt Plan B first."

And there, he believed, was the truth behind the sudden coming of Turk soldiers. The Turks had surely schemed this moment. Dagul had vowed to deliver money for a sizeable haul of the cargo. That no cash had yet been put in his hands suggested the ex-MIT operatives had duped him.

They wanted the mother lode all for themselves.

"Colonel Dagul, was it not you who told me to trust no one outside of us?"

"That was before what I fear is a full-scale attack by a man I know will bring the mountain down on our heads."

Mohammed watched as the Turks fanned out, his AK-47 ready to begin spraying them should their American M-16s lift an inch his direction. "Your man, Colonel."

"That much is true, but you knew this. I have attempted to hold him back, pledging some form of negotiation."

"Stalling, you mean."

"If you allow me to contact him, I can perhaps work out a deal…"

"For whom?" he asked, watching the Turk's gaze narrow.

"You are willing then to allow us to be killed and all we've worked for to be seized in a moment of insanity?"

Mohammed weighed the argument. They could defend the cave, his fighters already positioning themselves around the glacier, but only up to a point before the fearsome Apache began churning up bodies with its 30 mm Chain gun and Hellfire missiles. Perhaps it was worth the attempt to reach a settlement with the advancing Turks.

"We'll try it your way, Colonel Dagul. But, be warned, should they attempt to take what is mine by force, should I feel even remotely threatened, you and your men will be the first ones I kill."

"FIRE ONLY ON MY SIGNAL. Go for the tail and main rotors."

It was a judgment call, based for the most part on self-preservation, but hatred and the hunger for revenge ran a close second.

The Turks were coming.

Truth be told, Murat Ghirghulz knew he was overpowered by primal blood lust at first sight of the sleek, shark-shaped Apache gunship as it sliced through the mist, a stone's throw out over the ravine. He wasn't sure how much longer he could still his trigger finger on the RPG-7.

He was crouched behind a row of rock shaped like wolf's fangs, when the warbird sailed on. It went surging for some higher point, vanishing into the white plumes in seconds flat, but the buzzing of rotors remained strong. It told him the flying shark was sticking close, perhaps hovering now, this winged predator searching for meat as the two-man crew checked their heat seeking screens and sensors. His point men, he knew, had claimed a roost, another hundred feet higher and to the east, hunkered along a narrow ledge. Enveloped inside the mist, with darkness quickly falling, they were near invisible, even to his own eyes.

Ghosts with sniper rifles, AK-47s and RPG-7s.

Straining to hear beyond the Apache's whining bleat, he tried to distinguish between the blowing wind and what he believed were more sets of rotors, deeper below, farther to the west. They were holding, waiting for the Apache, he suspected, to either draw fire or blast them off the side of the mountain. He knew the Turks had at least two Black Hawks, as he gave his men the nod to arm themselves with their RPGs, hand signaling for them to be ready to unload when the gunships appeared. Against the armor-plated Apache, assault rifles, he knew, were as useless as blowing spitballs.

But if there were M-60 door gunners on the Black Hawks...

He lifted his radio, then clearly made out the whapping buzz, climbing, rotor wash sweeping away mist, as the sleek warbird rose slowly across the far side of the ravine. There were two more sleek dark shapes, he spotted, holding their position, dipping and yawing, whether from wind gusts or the pilots working the throttles, he couldn't say.

Ghirgulz was a second away from telling his point men to fire at will when an explosion blossomed across the ravine.

THE MOMENT SEIZED Tariq Khaballah. It was as if the RPG-7 had an angry life all its own, his finger taking up slack on the trigger.

One second, he was reporting to Mohammed, hunkered behind the slab of stone on the north edge overlooking the ravine, the next moment the Apache gunship was roaring his direction. Memories of what he had seen the dreaded warbird do to his fellow Iraqis was the catalyst, he supposed, that drove him to—

Then it vanished into the clouds.

He cursed the flying demon, urging it to reappear, but it stayed hidden in the mist. Then he set his sights on the Black Hawk as it ascended, hugging what looked like an outcrop, jutting into the mist like a giant stone pillar. He didn't care if they were Turks—rumor being of late, though, an American force was in the region—his mind raging with bitter recall of how many fellow Iraqis he'd witnessed shredded by the American gunships.

He rose, attempting to line up a better angle on the shadowy form of the Black Hawk. Just as he squeezed the trigger, his feet slipped on a patch of ice, the warhead sailing away as he pitched backward. Howling, as jagged stone stabbed him in the back, he glimpsed the fireball erupt over the Black Hawk.

25

The blast nearly sent Braden tumbling out the door. Gauging the free fall was anybody's guess, as the mist shot up for his bugging eyes, but he figured a thousand-plus-foot plunge, easy, to the floor of the gorge.

No thanks. Not after all he endured. He was holding on for number one.

His free hand shooting out, Braden grabbed onto the harness that held his M-60 door gunner, Cronin, in place. The spiderweb clutch at the last instant spared him the swan dive. Whoever was howling wild—the load of prisoners, he suspected—served only to infuriate him, safe as they were, deep in the belly of the Black Hawk. Two close shaves in as many days, but why should the rat screw end, here and now?

"Shut the hell up!" he roared at the prisoners, lurching back, HK swinging toward the jumble of orange jumpsuits as dust and smoke boiled through the hatchway.

Braden then heard the pilot bellow for everyone to hold on, as he pitched the gunship to starboard, before dropping them hard and fast. Again, several of the militants were crying out, their anger and panic swelling the fuselage with an unholy racket, as they banged into the walls or ate the floor.

Oh, yes, he had expected trouble before they went wheels up here, but all hell was breaking loose, and in a déjà vu of terror, blood and thunder that boiled his blood with a demonic fury. From what Locklin had informed him, moments ago, it sounded like he needed a scorecard to track all the players, but between the mist and every nook, cranny and crevice that could hide shooters like ghosts they would play hell to catch up and dish it back. The only upside was everyone outside their strike force was fair game.

That damn sure included the American special ops cavalry they knew was on the way. If they were made by their own—and he had his suspicions who had rallied the black ops—and tagged for termination…

Braden suspected it was about to become every man for himself.

Good enough.

He knew how to play that game with the best of them.

Having detailed his own problems during his call to Locklin when they landed in Sierra Leone for the first of two refueling stops in Africa—a tense period all by its lonesome as he was forced to unload fifty grand and when their contact there was already greased, supposedly, in advance—the Company black op had warned him the situation on his end was growing dicier with each passing hour. They needed to hit, hard and quick, secure the cargo, bail Turkey. Easier said than done, but if he wanted easy, Braden figured he would have simply vanished into the jungle back in Brazil, shacked up with a native girl and buried the now seriously depleted war chest in the earth for a rainy day.

And it was raining, all right, he found, pure hellfire and brimstone.

Cronin was blazing away, the M-60 barking out a storm of 7.62 mm NATO rounds, but at what Braden couldn't determine, unless he shuffled closer to the hatch. Rounds were drumming the fuselage, however, as he believed he spotted armed figures, cloaked in fur and rags, hunched and firing from above, staggered down some fanged precipice.

Kurds.

He was hoping the Apache crew had the good sense to start unloading the Hellfires or they were going down in a ball of flames. A second later, as several rounds screamed off the floorboards, one of the prisoners cried out, clutching a hole in his chest and toppling over. The south wall above and beyond the Black Hawk began lighting up with marching fireballs. The avalanche of rubble and bodies was sure to follow, as thunder pealed on, Braden bellowing at his pilot, "Back it up and get us up above this mess before we get slammed into the mountain or blown to hell!"

WHETHER ONE SIDE or the other had fired a shot in panic or anger, Faisal Mohammed couldn't say, and not that it mattered any longer.

He was running up to the lip overlooking the western edge of the glacier, eight of his fighters fanning out and dropping for cover behind boulders and slabs of stone, when he took in the terrible pounding the Apache was laying on the south face of the ravine.

Kurd turf, according to his spotters.

The winged demon was becoming more visible as rotor wash sliced gaps in the mist, and there was no mistaking the flames its rocket pods breathed as he saw Hellfires streak away, slamming the Kurds at near point-blank range. While explosions raked the precipice and he made out what appeared to be torn stick figures sailing away from the fireballs, other gunships seemed to gyrate below the Apache, backing up, spinning, then rising as if to escape the rain of rock and mangled bodies.

"We need to load as much as we can—*now!*—and fly out of here before they land on the glacier!"

Mohammed squeezed his eyes shut, felt the rage burn every nerve ending, as Colonel Dagul screamed out his demand again. It was clear now what was happening. The Turks had come to slaughter them, and clean out the store.

"Then go!" Mohammed told him, then waited as the colonel wheeled, barking orders at his contingent, the group breaking away in a jog.

And Mohammed made his decision. It was his mountain, it was his stockpile. It was his game to win, or lose. If there was no tomorrow, why should there be any reason to live on, other than to stand his ground?

He called the names of two of his closest fighters, as he swung his AK-47 around, drew a bead on Dagul's back and held back on the trigger.

THE BURLAP SATCHEL of warheads went with his tumble down the slope. Ghirgulz heard the wrath of the Apache's Hellfires, the explosions loud enough to spike his brain in two, senses so cleaved the sum total of pain and shock threatened to cut loose what was churning in his stomach from any orifice. Shock waves—like the seismic detonations from earthquakes often felt in Turkey—and flying rubble, what he figured were dismembered limbs slapped off his face and head, as he tasted blood on his lips and took the wet sting in the eyes.

But he was still going, in one piece, from what he could determine. If only he could turn the tide of battle. But how?

An invisible force alone, it seemed, was strong enough to almost hurl him off the edge of the precipice, as the rain of stone, blood and body parts kept falling.

Would that thunder of hell ever cease?

Once he stopped screaming from the pain lancing his senses, he looked out over the ravine, spotted the dark blur like a rapidly ascending wraith as the Black Hawk shot up, vanishing higher into the mist. Above, making out the howls of pain and rage, he heard the chatter of AK-47s, cursing his own men for fools for thinking they could drop the Apache with autofire. Then he caught the rumble of more explosions, saw the fire clouds peppering the distant north wall. A few of his fighters, then, clinging to stay in the battle, throwing RPG warheads at the gunship, but missing.

Just one well-placed round, he knew, was all it would take.   .

He dug into his bag, fisting a warhead as the blasts kept on coming, meshing in a world of fire that seemed to hammer down right on top of him.

BRADEN FEARED WHAT WAS coming next would prove more disastrous than the close shave he'd just ducked. The Apache was rising, climbing above but nearly on top of them. The damn flight crew was miming his evasive move, but putting their own chopper in the scissoring paths of warheads flying up from the precipice as the Kurds tracked on, winging missiles away, crazy bastards aware there was no tomorrow.

And the Apache was taking RPG hits. Wherever the other Black Hawks were in the formation was not his concern, since the world he watched was ready to crush them to shredded pulp.

As Cronin kept sweeping the precipice with M-60 lead storms, Braden roared at the pilot to keep climbing. "Get above those shooters and drop us off!"

They were rising, the world tilting to aft, when one or several of the Kurds scored big time.

Braden ripped loose a stream of obscenities as the tail rotor was sheared off, two or maybe three more fireballs dismembering the main rotor. Cronin was shedding the harness, ready to bail as the Black Hawk swung out over what looked like a tabletop above the Kurd shooters. From the corner of his eye, he spotted prisoners and his own commandos rushing forward. The thought crossed his mind he might need to hold them back with a burst of fire or the stampede might knock him out the door before he was ready to leap, but the helicopter was already in a whirling dervish.

And an errant Hellfire parted the dissipating clouds, coming on, in his face.

Braden beat the stampede out the door, jumping, staring at the tableland. Twenty or thirty feet, he hoped there was enough snow to cushion his crash landing, no jutting rock prepared to break him in two. He was vaguely aware of Cronin hollering in his ear, free-falling beside him, as the explosion roared above and superheated wind came screaming from the sky.

MURAT GHIRGULZ KNEW he was finished. If possible, though, he wished to take a few more of the enemy with him in his dying breath, a pyrrhic victory, at least, denying as many of them as he could of what was being snatched from him in death.

Something had been hurled from one of the two blasts, and it was impaled deep through his ribs, angling up, into his chest. The sky appeared to be on fire, wreckage and stone hailing around his outstretched form, the screaming wind so hot as it boiled over him it seemed to suck the air out of his lungs. Breathing was nearly impossible, as blood gushed up his throat, spewing forth in a blackish tint that puddled the snow to melting slime before his eyes.

Somehow, call it sheer willpower—or perhaps hatred of the fact he was doomed to fail in his quest to create an independent Kurdistan with the blackmail of WMD—he rolled up on his good side, AK-47 in hand. And the gates of hell, he found, had erupted wide open, along and above the precipice, the damned in full wailing flight.

Whether they were his men or the ones who had leaped from the Black Hawk before the missile plowed into the cockpit was impossible to tell. They were engulfed in flames, maybe six in all, about half of the burning scarecrows rolling down the slope, shrieking as they thrashed in the snow in hopes of extinguishing their shrouds of fire. Another three human comets simply jumped over the edge, their hideous wails whipped away with both the plummet and a wrenching noise that warned him the sky was again falling.

Looking up, he spied two shapes in orange jumpsuits, clinging to the edge of a promontory that stretched in for the tableland.

Human flies.

He'd take it.

Choking back blood and bile, he managed to squeeze off a burst of autofire. He thought he stitched both flies on the wall, in the legs or lower back, but couldn't be positive, as the flaming hull of the downed Black Hawk thundered off the lip near his targets in a shower of fire and flying wreckage, then came plunging to bury him where he lay.

26

The Executioner discovered they were late for the beginning of the war for the WMD, suspected the blame would land on his head if it fell apart for their side. Other than slogging through a conspiracy slowly unraveling around him with each body, dodging bullets and chasing his own bad guys nearly halfway around the planet, there were no good excuses, even if he was so inclined to explain himself. And only the Presidential Directive in the hands of what he read as a stewing Major General Eugene Thomas kept him from sitting on the bench back at Incirlik.

They were there now, bottom line, six gunships total, and surging into the gorge. Nose up, they were climbing, rapidly grabbing higher altitude, Thomas barking for as much over Bolan's com link, as small-arms fire from the Turk convoy hundreds of feet below broke out. But the flying armada was sailing on, out of range of everything save a surface-to-air missile. That show of force indicated to Bolan that America's only NATO ally in the Middle East had more than a few militants, even traitors in uniform in the neighborhood, willing to go the distance. He figured Thomas could always mop them up later with one of his two Apaches—since it would take several hours at the very least for the convoy to reach the glacier in question—once the WMD was secured.

Bolan had plenty of questions about Operation Thor, but

decided to let the fighting piece together the whole puzzle. The M-16/M-203 combo was locked and loaded, his tried and proved side arms ready as backup, webbing hung with spare clips and grenades.

In some way, he supposed it was fitting to nail down the WMD mystery, once and for all, in a land that was the crossroads of history, the bridge between East and West. Where countless civilizations from the ancient Hittites to the Ottoman Empire had risen and fallen. Where mass migrations of Indo-Europeans and scores of invading armies had left their mark, everything from culture and architecture to bloodlines. Where, yes, the Great Flood had deposited the Ark somewhere, allegedly, high up the mountain, where the snow and the cloud cover was eternal, hiding whatever the truth. And now, in the new century, he thought, one of the most horrific of potential scourges, albeit man-made, could plunge an entire region...

The truth would soon enough reveal itself.

Still, Bolan wondered, why distribute gas masks and atropine injectors to counteract the effects of exposure to nerve gas, with no sign of a HAZMAT team among the strike force, nor even a hint that such was on standby? Nerve agents attacked both through the respiratory system and skin absorption. There was no guarantee his blacksuit—with double-layered thermals beneath—black-gloved hands and nylon hood would spare him the lethal touch of VX. Not only that, but if this sorcerers's brew was similar in chemical composition to what he'd witnessed eating men alive as if they'd been dipped in acid, only a NASA-customized spacesuit would save him. And why did the general hint he already had a good idea where the stockpile was tucked away, but was tight-lipped on how he knew all of this?

There were three intelligence operatives from the Turk MIT on-board the General's Black Hawk. Bolan suspected they had paved the way in, from what little he gathered during the briefest of combat briefs he'd ever sat through. Very little, though, surprised the soldier when it came to black ops. Given his experience in spookdom, where all sides often jealously guarded intelligence and informants, and where very little was actually as it appeared...

Which was why he was flying solo at his insistence, the two Stony Man blacksuits in the cockpit, Michaels manning the mother of all Gatling guns in the open hatchway.

While the flying armada consisted of three Black Hawks and two Apaches, Bolan personal choice of gunship was the black helicopter special. Informed by his crew the hybrid Huey-Black Hawk was built for speed and maneuverability after a preflight check, the armament was what turned the corner in Bolan's decision. The M-61 Vulcan Gatling gun in 20 mm was mounted on a short-legged tripod, welded into the floorboards. The revolving six-barreled cannon could spew up to 6,000 armor-piercing rounds per minute from the linkless feed in the storage drum. With the weapon in the capable hands of Michaels, the Executioner was more than confident he had all the cover from above he would require.

The rest, when he hit the ground, was up to him.

There was no point running enemy numbers through his mind, as he saw the flaming shells of two downed gunships illuminating the mist below, dozens of bodies—or what was left of them—strewed down a precipice, more certain to be pancaked on the gorge floor. The good general claimed a hundred and change in shooters, between the renegade Turks, their American counterparts and the terrorists on the glacier, with a possibility some Kurds might show up for the big event. Oxygen bottles were optional, but Thomas indicated they weren't going much higher than two thousand feet.

So much for a potential Ark sighting.

Part of the team, more or less, but Bolan was braced for anything.

He began wondering if Braden had even made the scene when he suddenly spotted the commotion on the narrow plateau above the carnage spread around the downed Black Hawk.

He saw maybe a half-dozen men in orange jumpsuits, limping or stumbling up a snowy embankment, several of them prying weapons from the hands of bodies littering the way. With darkness falling over the mountain, it was near impossible to positively identify another group of armed stragglers lurching onto the plateau.

And it hit Bolan again.

That instinctive tug, as if he was being guided to the next battlefront by some unseen force, reaching out and grabbing him.

The Executioner relayed new orders to his blacksuits.

JABIR NAHAB FELT the panic rising around him. No, he corrected, it was a mindless rage that had gripped the three men he assumed were in charge, edging fast toward murder.

He listened as they screamed at one another about how to proceed. The Turk general was torn between his radioman and the bellowing of the ones he knew as Locklin and Hawke. The Turk demanded they wait for reinforcements, look poised to begin unloading his M-16 on the Americans who likewise, he sensed, were on the edge of cutting loose with their weapons. A do or die stand.

And where would that leave him? he wondered.

Whatever had happened back in the gorge had demolished their strategy. Now, at their moment of impending failure and doom, they were ready to turn on one another like wild beasts, backs to the corner. If they started shooting, he knew he had no choice but to attempt a bull rush through the falling bodies, a headlong dive out the door, then hurl himself at the mercy of his fellow holy warriors.

He'd explain himself, about leading the infidels here. He offered a silent prayer to Allah they showed mercy. After all, hadn't he suffered the worst at the hands of the infidels beatings and such? Surely, it was preordained he was there, breathing free air, ready, stronger and more determined than ever to take up the sword of jihad. Assuming the infidel problem was solved, he could lead them to countless contacts, fighters who were more than willing to drive the imperial occupation force of barbarians from all of the Middle East. There were freedom fighters in the Gaza Strip, the West Bank, Pakistan and Afghanistan, as far away as Indonesia…

They were landing on the glacier, regardless of the heated argument, where he knew the stockpile was hidden deep in a cave at the northern edge. As they touched down with a jolt, he saw Locklin pluck a mike off the wall, stab a button. His senses rocked by their shouting, rotor wash and his own cold fear, Nahab barely made out the demand Locklin boomed over the glacier from the loudspeaker. He wanted to deal, money in hand, for a portion of the stockpile. There was no need for a shooting war. They could negotiate. He was sending out one of their own to talk.

And just who might that be? Nahab bitterly thought, staring into the blackness beyond the open doorway, braced for an RPG bombardment that would blow him into a thousand pieces. Then Locklin wheeled on him, grabbed him by the shoulder and snarled, "Come here. You're going to be my messenger. You're going to tell your boys we're not leaving without a big fat sweet chunk of that stockpile. Money or bullets, they can decide. Everyone will die here, no one gets squat unless they deal with us."

Nahab hesitated, then Locklin slung him out the door where he pitched to the ground, face plowing down into snow.

Beyond the whine of the gunship's rotors, he strained his ears, but heard only ominous silence. There was no movement anywhere on the glacier, but he knew they were out there, everywhere, perhaps thirty fighters all with AKs and RPGs poised to unload. Locklin was barking for him to get moving. He shivered and got to his feet. With the snow swirling in his face, he shuddered forward, decided to raise his arms.

Surrender. Negotiate.

What else could he do?

He was looking around, sensed he was being watched, when two armed shadows came leaping over the edge of an upraised horizontal slab of rock, no more than a dozen feet in front of him. And Nahab froze at the sight of the suicide bombers as they landed, and charged.

There was screaming and cursing from the Black Hawk at the sight of the martyrs, their torsos wrapped with canisters, and Nahab—having heard the rumors—suspected what was the payload they were about to unleash. The stammer of combined autofire, his enemies leaping from the doorway behind and the horrifying reality of what was surging into their blazing weapons jolted sudden electricity through his limbs. He was bolting left, northbound, trying to put lightning distance between himself and the horror he knew was on the way, when white-hot pain tore down his side.

Nahab fell to the snow, knew he'd been shot.

He looked back, saw the martyrs forging into the pounding wave of bullets, remote boxes in hand. Crabbing ahead, mind ripped by silent screams, he heard the thunder peal its nightmare doom from behind. They were shrieking like banshees, weapons now silent, as images of how they were dying propelled him harder, faster in his scramble. He cried for deliverance from Allah, hoping he was spared from the obscene injustice of it all.

Then the hideous chemical odor washed over his senses and trapped the scream in his throat as the vapor flooded into his lungs.

Then the instant everyone seemed, the doors slammed.

27

The ghosts of battles past were calling out to him, howling in rage, groaning in misery of their mortal wounds, hungry to drag him down into the abyss. Braden believed he could hear the angry cry of the dead and the damned in the wind, feel their pain in the hot blood running from the deep gash on his scalp as he ripped off the hood and flung it away.

Failure.

Death.

And the signs of doom were everywhere. Kurds. Arabs. His own black-clad marauders, the team down to three—make that four, including his angry war dog hide—and they weren't in the best of shape. Mauled and torn. Scorched from fire, moaning and cursing as they trudged, bleeding in the snow, weapons ready.

He saw bodies and severed limbs, puddled guts and gore wherever he navigated across the plateau. Smoking black mummies melting the snow on the promontory behind. Incredibly, he found six, maybe more of the Arabs had made the jump, a few of them crying out to him, as if he was their savior.

As if he gave a damn.

Fuck 'em.

Com link and radio gone with the blast or ripped from his head by shrapnel during the leap, he had no way to call Locklin and Hawke for a pick up. They would climb the high ground, make the glacier.

Kick some heavy ass.

He shrugged off the hellish memories of Afghanistan, Brazil and now this debacle, vectoring parallel to a wash, maybe eight feet deep by his reckoning. The pitiful bastards behind were about to be treated to a subgun burst, Braden thinking he should put them out of his misery. But the Arabs had armed themselves with discarded Kurd AK-47s. He heard the whining of rotor blades. Wheeling, hoping it was Locklin—

Then that heartbeat of joy was dashed to hell when the black helicopter sliced through the clouds and the door gunner cut loose with the heavy metal thunder of a Gatling gun. He was jumping into the wash, howling with rage, as he glimpsed at least two of his men obliterated into dark blossoming clouds by what he had to assume were some major league armor-piercing rounds.

He left them to disintegrate.

And he had to laugh.

The cavalry had arrived, all but sealing his doom.

Well, he wasn't going down, at least not without a roar of lions. He found Cronin had made cover, then the commando hollered, "Grenade!"

Spotting the steel egg as it bounced up damn near in Cronin's lap, Braden was hauling himself the other way when the lethal baseball blew. He was airborne on the tails of fire, heard himself scream as flying steel piranhas chewed up his backside.

The stink of cordite and blood swam in his nose, as he landed on a slab of rock. The horrible racket of that Gatling gun thundered on, Arabs on the plateau getting shoved through the meat grinder. Smoke drifted over his head, boiling down the wash, as he grimaced against fresh waves of fire racing down his back. He sensed a presence and hauled in his weapon as the tall shadow seemed to materialize out of the darkness and the smoke. He was bringing up the HK 33, when he hesitated, recognizing the manner in which the black wraith moved, made out those familiar icy blue eyes burning back at him from behind the hangman's hood.

Stone.

And he sounded off a final bitter chuckle, finger taking up slack on the HK's trigger but Washington's black op SOB opened fire, drilling the ultimate and last failure through his chest.

ZHABAT WEPT. It wasn't so much from the pain, but the horror he found between his legs. Someone had shot him. He raged at the unknown source of his nightmare, when he'd clung to the ledge of the outcrop. One or several rounds through his ass, it didn't matter. Whoever the devil, he had blown off his manhood, balls and all.

He screamed as he reached down, saw his intestines sliding through his fingers, the yellow-red-brown mass like gruesome serpents in the glowing halo of firelight.

Oh, Allah, how could this be? Why?

Blubbering, he crawled through the snow, trailing tears and blood, crying out in a voice of pure agony and anguish, demanding to know of Allah why he hadn't left him behind in Brazil, spared him this most shameful of fates.

He was jolted by screams other than his own. Out on the plateau, he saw his brother jihadists being dismembered by the furious thunder and lightning of a massive machine gun with spinning barrels. He stared up the black helicopter, the doomsday weapon and the black-clad demon manning it. He was frozen by the sight of bodies erupting like giant gore-filled balloons, men literally blown to bits of meat and gristle out of their shoes.

The roar of that revolving weapon, the pounding rotor wash sliced white-hot agony through his brain.

He screamed, vomited, then slithered back to the relative safety of the outcrop, pried an AK-47 from the hand of severed arm along the way.

The trumpet of doom abruptly stopped. He heard the sound of his bitter weeping, retching, spitting. He searched the plateau, peering into the wafting spirals of smoke and mist. The chopper rose.

He was sure he spotted a big armed shadow, somewhere in the smoke, believed it was headed his way, but the figure was there, then gone, as if the pall had absorbed him into invisibility.

"Help me! I'm wounded!" he shouted. *"Help me!"*

And he sobbed on, lifted the AK-47.

The shadow parted the smoke to his right, the massive assault rifle with fixed grenade launcher rising. He heard the weapon roar.

IT WAS A BAD WAY TO DIE. The way he understood it, recalling how his science crew and weapons engineers had explained the effects during litmus tests on Kurd subjects, a fifteen-syllable enzyme in the nervous system—acetyl-something—was fried on first whiff. Nervous system in vapor lock, there was instant heart and respiratory meltdown, though he'd witnessed such fierce convulsions a victim could break his own bones as he suffocated, burning up from within in mindless agony. Colorless, odorless and invisible, a dollop the size of a pinhead could kill a dozen men within minutes, depending on wind, grouping of victims and such. The trick was prolonging the potency of the agent once it was dispersed. Requisite thickeners were added to slow evaporation. There were nonpersistent and persistent agents, he knew, the former made useless by the simple donning of a HAZ-

MAT suit, the latter capable of contaminating an area for days.

He knew the VX dropping the enemy on the glacier was somewhere in-between.

Rising from behind his boulder, Mohammed could fairly assume he owned the mountain. He liked the sound of that, as he rolled it back through his head. Mohammed of the Mountain. Careful, he cautioned himself. The arrogance of the enemy had gotten them killed. And negotiate? For what? Even if they had all the money in the world, he wasn't about to be duped by their treachery.

Fools. Dead ones at that.

The second Black Hawk vanished in a roiling fireball as his fighters slammed the gunship with a slew of RPG warheads, blasting it all over the glacier, nothing but flying, smoking wreckage and minced human flesh smearing the snow and ice. Between rotor wash, wind gusts and explosions, they were out of harm's way of VX extermination, though he caught a faint whiff of what smelled like pesticide.

He was walking down the incline, pleased with the utter destruction of fools who would dare believe they could deceive him when the first of several explosions tore through the glacier, freezing him in midstride. They wore four gunships, according to his spotters, the Apache and the last Black Hawk down, so what in the—

Mohammed began charging for the cave entrance, shouting at his troops to fall back, secure the stockpile, when he spotted two Apaches streaking in from the southwest, Chain guns roaring, Hellfires flaming away from rocket pods.

THE STOREKEEPERS didn't stand a chance.

Hellfires, Chain gun and Black Hawk minigun annihilation were pounding the slopes on all points around the glacier, mangled figures flying, or sliced and diced where they stood their ground.

Not a hope in the hell where they were going.

The Executioner bounded out the door, quarter-inch spikes on his combat boots digging into the ice pack as he began picking off targets with his M-16, dropping two hardmen out of the gate, twin whirling dervishes that dropped out of sight behind snow-covered boulders now slick with crimson. With Thomas already alerted to his arrival, Bolan left Michaels to a sweep on his six. Platoon strength blacksuits, he saw, began mopping up on foot as they chased down rabbits or shot the terrorists where they roosted.

Gas mask on, Bolan marched double-time for the cave, as he found squad-strength blacksuits with protective covering penetrating the natural armory provided by the brute force of Mother Nature. The glacier swathed in firelight, visibility was not a problem, as the Executioner picked out two more enemy guardians and waxed them where they fired, one o'clock, above the maw.

Down and out.

Sporadic bursts trailed the warrior into the cave. He patched through to Thomas, rolling on, as the strike force fanned out before him. Moments later, as he closed on a huge bowl-shaped depression, the general intercepted him before he descended into an armory that would lay to rest the mystery of the WMD.

It was quite the cache. First look, and Bolan figured a few thousand shells of various size and shape.

When Bolan saw the bald black man strip off his gas mask, he followed the all-clear.

Thomas appeared his usual seething self as he barked into his com link, then turned on Bolan. "Nice of you to make the show, Colonel Stone."

The Executioner glanced away from Thomas, saw a three-man team, trailed by the Turk MIT threesome sweep past and descend into the WMD armory. One of the men had a backpack strapped around his shoulders. Bolan began to understand the absence of HAZMAT teams.

Unbelievable, he thought. All the dead, the innocent, the good and the wicked, gone to the next world, whether to seek out or cover the truth. Kicking down one door after another to get to the truth himself. In the here and now, at the end of the road where the answers stood before him. And it was all destined to be nuked up the mountain.

It felt wrong.

Bolan watched as the man set the pack down in front of the first row of standing shells and ripped away its Velcro covering. He then inserted a key, a series of red-lit numbers flashing up. Bolan sounded a grim chuckle as the man began punching in the access code.

"You find something amusing about all this?" Thomas growled.

"Is this a political or a military call?"

"Both. Neither. I got my orders, straight from CENTCOM, if you care to read them."

Bolan let the M-16 hang by his leg. "I'll take your word on that."

"Damn straight you will. I don't know who you are or how you got dipped in presidential honey, but it's my party from here on. I suggest you evac. Plenty of time, thirty minutes and counting as of this moment, for you to make our refuel pit stop on the way back to Incirlik. Then this mountain goes up and buries this garbage with the help of eight kilotons."

Bolan slowly shook his head, grunted.

"You got a problem with this?"

"I have lots of problems, General."

"Don't make me one of them. What you see about to happen here is something you will take to the grave with you—how that happens is up to you. Understood?"

"Like you said—it's your party," Bolan told the man, and walked away.

"COLONEL, IT'S HOME BASE, sir."

They were soaring over the gorge, about a thousand feet up, Bolan taking in the shellacking being dumped on the convoy by the Apaches when Michaels informed him Brognola was on the sat link. Apparently Operation Thor wasn't taking any prisoners.

Dirty war, damn right. And the god of thunder was about twenty-six minutes away from burying the truth.

Slowly, the Executioner turned away from the saturation Hellfire bombing and Chain gun lightning that dropped the hammer on the convoy. He almost couldn't wait to tell the big Fed the news of the ages, pretty sure, though, Brognola wouldn't be the least bit surprised about the nuclear burial.

Slipping on the headphones, Bolan heard Brognola say, "There's been some rather suspicious developments on my end. By the way, your fast taxi will be an SR-71 Blackbird. Don't ask me how our lady does it, but she rustled it up, out of retirement. It will be sitting on the ground at Incirlik. A KC-10 tanker is on standby in England for midair refueling over the Atlantic. At Mach 3 you should be back in record."

Bolan did the logistics. Within hours, he'd be back on U.S. soil.

"One other thing, Striker, before I fill you in."

"Tell me it's good news for a change."

"I don't know how good it is, but the Man has given you everything you asked for. You do know what part of that means, don't you?"

Bolan did, but said it anyway. "If what I think is about to happen does, in fact, happen, you'll be in charge of the country."

"I said it before, and I'll say it again—I hope to God you're wrong."

And so did Bolan. It was only a nagging suspicion, growing darker, gnawing at him deeper with each corpse left in his wake, but if he was right...

God save America.

28

It was going to be a beautiful day in the neighborhood, Durham thought, closing on the two Secret Service agents standing post at the doors to the Oval Office.

Check that.

Beautiful night under the White House roof, a sterling reborn America coming with the dawn. It may be the dead of night, but by the time the sun rose over Washington a new America, meeting his terms and conditions, would be announced to the nation.

And the President would be his personal press secretary, dictating his terms to the masses.

Or else there would be hell to pay in Washington, a hundred thousand times 9/11 or more.

Gringelt and Robinson on his wings, with Griswald at his elbow, Durham watched as the Secret Service agents reached to open the door. The emergency meeting had been called hours ago when Durham announced he had discovered the source of the leaks. On hand would be the National Security Adviser and top aides, the Chairman of the Joint Chiefs and the chief of staff.

How sweet it was.

"Don't trouble yourselves, gentlemen," Durham said.

On cue, Gringelt and Robinson shed the Beretta M-9s from shoulder rigging and shot the men in the face, point-blank. He heard Griswald make some gagging noise, as he bulled into the most powerful room on the planet, freeing his own Beretta.

Time to take the crown.

Durham smiled at the confusion and fear that greeted him, his weapon aimed at the President as he rose from behind his desk. "Sit down! Or I'll put one through this asshole's face," he snarled, shoving the muzzle at the chief of staff. They were hurling outrage, a babble of voices, someone cursing him.

Until Durham slammed a right cross off the jaw of the chief of staff, dropped him square on the Presidential Seal.

That settled them, he saw, the pig squirming all over the floor, dribbling blood, hacking all over the most important symbol on Earth.

"God knows, that felt good," Durham said, then kicked the chief of staff in the ribs. "I've been aching to do that since I first laid eyes on this ass-kissing toad."

Quickly Gringelt and Robinson shed their coats and shirts, unfastened their vests. Tearing off the Velcro, they went to work, shaping then fixing softball-sized gobs of plastique. Doors, windows, the walls and finally the Man's desk. All primed, Durham bellowed for everyone to shut their mouths, all questions would be answered in due course. He punched in the numbers on his cell phone, saw the red lights flash on the primers.

Outstanding.

All he needed to do was punch SEND. Another set of numbers tapped in and the second digital readout would flash GO. SEND twice, and Washington, D.C., would be a smoking radioactive crater. Oh, but hats off to the geek wizards of the National Security Agency who invented such high-tech toys.

Pure genius.

"Are you insane! What is the meaning of this?" the President shouted.

"This is treason, for which you will hang," the chairman said, and Durham shoved him down into his seat, pulling back on the urge to shoot him between the eyes.

"Sir, listen to me and obey," Durham told the President. "You are no longer in charge of the Free World. I will crush you before God and the human race, should you disobey me. I will skin you alive on national television if you do not kiss my ass. You are allowed two phone calls—sir. One will be to the Secret Service. Should anyone attempt some heroic charge into this room, there is enough C-4 here to blow us all clear to the Potomac. That in mind, should you force my hand," he said and laughed, "all tours of the mansion will clearly be canceled tomorrow morning and every morning after."

"You're mad."

"And you're going to be executed," Durham told the Chairman. "If one more foolish word comes out of you." He pointed his weapon at the President. "Call two is a freebie. Call whomever you want. Your wife, your priest, your mistress. Oh, and one other thing, people. There is a ten-kiloton nuke somewhere in this city." He smiled as the chairman groaned, the chief of staff scraped himself off the floor and the President cursed. "I have a list of demands and they do not include healthcare or welfare reform or gay marriage. All the little people are now under my boot heel, or, in my case, my wing tips. They will begin, each American household, by paying tribute to their new pharoah, cleaning out one-third of bank accounts, IRAs, stocks and bonds, and so forth. Cash will be accepted, as it will be mailed directly to this office in the coming day. We shall see, sir, how much your adoring voting public cares about your life. That, however, is only one item. Should anyone not meet my demands, I will incinerate Washington, D.C.," he told the President. "Please, the calls. And kindly do not wet your pants, or worse. I'm looking forward to sitting in that seat."

"You son of a bitch, I'll see you—"

"Sir! One last time, the calls, or I will start shooting."

Durham smiled at their outrage, as the President picked up his phone. Moments later, he heard the chief executive tell whoever was on the other end, "It's happening. And they have a nuclear device."

Durham didn't like the sound of that, but decided to let it go, as the President grunted, bobbing his head. Why waste time worrying when he owned the White House? The United States of America was a few hours away from becoming his personal kingdom.

THE SIXTY-PLUS-HOUR DELAY in delivering the suitcase to their room at the Embassy Suites had troubled Michael Rubin at first. He understood the need for caution, though, the two Russian military attachés had to cover their assets.

But it was happening, he knew, his pager vibrating minutes ago on his hip, telling him Durham had seized the Oval Office. A quick return page, and they were good to go.

Victory—military rule under martial law as dictated to the American masses by the Special Countermeasure Task Force—was as close as the morning's press conference. He could only imagine the show Durham had planned.

As the two buzz-cut Russians in black leather trench coats fiddled with the keyboards on their laptops, confirming their money had been electronically wired to wherever they kept the numbered account, Rubin pondered the immediate future. Just shy of the kilo tonnage that had wiped out Hiroshima, there was plenty of knockout punch. Enough, he knew, to vaporize the city, and beyond to Arlington and Falls Church, Virginia, to Bethesda, Maryland. Human beings, he envisioned, vanishing in the firestorm, leaving behind nothing more than shadows on the sidewalks. There would be hideous radioactive fallout, depending on the prevailing winds, burn and cancer victims crying out for death to relieve their

misery. Every house and seat of power in the city nothing but
an irradiated memory. There would be complete and total anarchy, as panicked herds jammed the interstates in a desperate attempt to flee for the safety of the countryside.

Naturally, it was only a last resort. The threat alone, or so
they all hoped, enough to hand them the keys to the kingdom.
Just in case, Rubin didn't intend to hang around and wait and
see if Durham pulled the trigger.

He was gently closing the suitcase, the Russians muttering something in their native tongue, when a loud bang blew
the door down. Rubin was leaping to his feet, the Russians
clawing inside their coats for pistols when the black-clad invader surged through the smoke. The big door crasher was
chopping down the Russians with a mini-Uzi, then swinging
his way as the bodies crashed off the table, bringing the laptops with them to the floor in smoke and sparking ruins.

"I wouldn't," the stranger warned him.

Rubin slowly pulled his hand away from his holstered
Beretta and raised his arms. He was vaguely aware of the hel-
meted armed shadows on the hallway landing, but the blue
eyes of the big invader had command of his full and terrified
attention.

"I want a deal," he stammered.

"Your life is only as good as a truthful tongue from this
moment on," the big invader told him. "That's your deal.
First, shut that thing down. Nod, if you intend to cooperate."

Rubin stared at the smoking muzzle aimed at his chest. He
nodded.

IT WAS CALLED the Doomsday Tunnel in the parlance of certain circles within the intelligence community. The Farm
knew of its existence, and Bolan had suspected Durham and
his team might, too.

Only Rubin—assuming he had been telling the truth about

the setup, the seizure and enemy numbers under the White House roof and beyond—claimed not even the President knew of the second shaft leading up to the Oval Office at the southwest corner. Apparently, it was recently engineered in the event of just such a nightmare scenario of a palace coup, or a terrorist. A straight shot, from the Pentagon, under the Potomac River, to the South Lawn. Bolan had the access code to Shaft Two committed to memory, certain it would be changed when he was done.

If he succeeded in pulling off the seemingly impossible.

A commando storm into the Oval Office.

Only Bolan was going in solo, the weight of the free world on his shoulders. If he failed...

He couldn't. He wouldn't.

Rubin, the ex-NSA counterterrorist storm tracker, had provided a gold mine of intel that was netting cannibals as the Executioner streaked on through the diesel-generator-powered gloom to destiny under the Oval Office roof.

How could this have happened? How much or how little did the President or those trusted with the nation's security around him really know?

Too many questions were hanging, but the political fall-out was not his concern.

Bolan was going all the way, no matter what, to save America.

Right then, a special Justice Department task force was rounding up what amounted to two squads of traitors around the metropolitan area, more to come, he was sure, when Brognola and his interrogators were finished. No Black Hawk from a private airfield in rural Virginia would whisk Durham and his VIP hostages to an undisclosed location to a private jet, then fly on, out of the country after the traitor announced his terms of national surrender to his will and whim at a dawn press conference.

Bolan sat, alone in the minitrain, as it rolled at what he assumed was several hundred feet beneath the city. Secretly, with the vice president far removed from the White House, the Speaker of the House was running the country. But Hal Brognola was given carte blanche.

The order had come straight from the President, who was now a hostage at gunpoint behind his own Resolute Desk.

Less than a minute later, the minitrain stopped beside a Marine toting an M-16, standing post by Shaft Two. Mini-Uzi in hand, the Executioner hopped out and hit the keypad on the wall. A pneumatic hiss, and Bolan was in the elevator car. Two hundred feet up, according to Pentagon brass. He tapped in another set of numbers to get him moving.

As he rose, the Executioner plucked a tear gas cannister from his webbing.

In a few moments, as he slipped the protective mask over his face, the Executioner would determine whether the free world remained free.

"IF IT MAKES YOU HAPPY, sir, go ahead and invite your favorite newsman for the morning announcement that the baton has been passed to me. Phony punk that he is, I've got a few choice words for him. That fat guy, and that blond yuppie punk, too. I wouldn't mind slapping his chubby cheeks, liberal piece of lying turd that he is. I bet he stops running his diarrhea mouth once I get hold of him," Durham said with a smile.

Why were they looking at him as if he was insane? Were these elected officials really that out of touch with reality? Didn't they see the future of the country was at stake? Couldn't they understand military rule was the only answer? Demographics, immigration, more affirmative action, homosexual marriage and stem cell research aside, America was dying, the wrath of God sure to come unless one good man stood up and said enough. Only a man—an angel of the Almighty—who could reach out and nearly touch divine wisdom and understanding could straighten out the immoral course before the barbarians stormed the gate. Only he could...

The explosion nearly bowled him down. There was a frozen second where the room boiled with the erupting cloud, but he knew the biting stink for tear gas for what it was, as he teetered, eyes watering, lungs filling up with vapor as the shroud swelled the Oval Office.

What the hell? The shaft of the Doomsday Tunnel was near under his feet, mined to go off if it was breached. How...?

Through the watery mist, gagging, Durham thought he spotted a tall dark figure in the southwest corner, believed he heard the stammer of a machine gun. He was reeling, gasping for air, grunts behind outblasting the choking when he realized—

Damn it!

He hit his knees, sweeping the Presidential Seal for his cell phone as the stammer of weapons fire tore through the thunder of the heartbeat in his ears.

There!

He snapped it up, on his feet, then spotted—

The shadow that was the President parted the mist, the Man vaulting over his desk, arms outstretched, eyes bugged with anger.

He was throwing his finger forward, zeroed on SEND despite the burning water in his eyes, when the full weight of the chief executive hammered him down, into the seal. The cell phone flying from his hand, he took a fist to the jaw. Somehow, powered by terror his thunder was being stolen, he drilled a foot into the President's gut, launched him into the desk.

He was sweeping the floor with hands fueled by panic, retching, near blind, when he scooped up the cell phone again.

Two stabs on SEND, and he didn't care as he felt the bullets bore through his spine.

Message sent.

Epilogue

No debrief, no handshake, no job well done. Not that the Executioner expected or much less wanted a pat on the back.

Mack Bolan walked out onto the South Lawn. He couldn't help but wonder where it all went from that night on. Who could say? The world was becoming a darker, stranger, scarier place...

Stow it. There would always be one more good fight left in him. The glue that held it all together was a few good folks willing to stand up and be accounted for when it came to facing down the most basic of all eternal questions, and mysteries.

Good versus evil.

No sooner was the last shot fired from his mini-Uzi then Griswald was in cuffs, and the Man was whisked away in the Doomsday Tunnel.

Job done, he reckoned.

For now.

Bolan stood his ground as the Black Hawk settled on the South Lawn. Good to be alive?

Damn right.

Hope for a better tomorrow?

Always.

Offer up a silent prayer of thanks and gratitude to the Universe?

Why not? What else was left, when the smoke cleared, the dust settled and the world went marching on to the beat of its own drum?

He knew, could feel he was wearing a thousand-yard-stare as he forged into the rotor wash, and saw Brognola step into the doorway.

Bolan looked at the big Fed and he felt the thousand-yard-stare fade into the ghost of another memory of another battle now that he was with a friend.